ALSO BY PAUL YOON

Snow Hunters
Once the Shore

THE MOUNTAIN

STORIES

PAUL YOON

SIMON & SCHUSTER

New York   London   Toronto   Sydney   New Delhi

Simon & Schuster
1230 Avenue of the Americas
New York, NY 10020

First Simon & Schuster hardcover edition August 2017

SIMON & SCHUSTER and colophon are registered trademarks of Simon & Schuster, Inc.

For information about special discounts for bulk purchases, please contact Simon & Schuster Special Sales at 1-866-506-1949 or business@simonandschuster.com.

The Simon & Schuster Speakers Bureau can bring authors to your live event. For more information or to book an event, contact the Simon & Schuster Speakers Bureau at 1-866-248-3049 or visit our website at www.simonspeakers.com.

Manufactured in the United States of America

10   9   8   7   6   5   4   3   2   1

Library of Congress Cataloging-in-Publication Data

Name: Yoon, Paul, author.
Title: The mountain : stories / Paul Yoon.
Description: New York : Simon & Schuster, 2017.
Identifiers: LCCN 2016054159| ISBN 9781501154089 (hardcover) |
ISBN 9781501154096 (paperback) | ISBN 9781501154102 (ebook).
Subjects: | BISAC: FICTION / Literary. | FICTION / Historical. | FICTION / General.
Classification: LCC PS3625.O54 A6 2017 | DDC 813/.6--dc23 LC record available at
https://lccn.loc.gov/2016054159

ISBN 978-1-5011-5408-9
ISBN 978-1-5011-5410-2 (ebook)

For Bill Clegg, Ralph Sneeden, and always, Laura

A body full of incomprehensible space.

—ADAM FOULDS

Then she takes off her shoes forever.

—JENNY ERPENBECK

CONTENTS

A WILLOW AND THE MOON

I.

It was once a sanatorium high up in the mountains. My mother worked there. In the summers I woke with her early and took the wooded trail near our home. She brought us breakfast, usually some bread with cold jam and butter, and halfway up the slope we found a spot with a view and rested.

In the valley there was the town and the distant river. On some days we could see the train come up from the city, blowing smoke into the sky. South of this was our house and the horse farm my father was employed by. Sometimes I could even see my father cross a paddock; I recognized his strange gait, from when a horse kicked his hip before I was born.

He came from a family of farriers. The house was one we rented from a wealthy Dutchman whom I never saw. It had four rooms on one floor. Our most valuable possession was a piano my mother owned. She used to play, before the first war. She had come to America to perform in a concert hall in Manhattan.

Her name was Joséphine. She was from France. She was supposed to be in the city for only a week. One afternoon she went to a market and my father was there, trying to sell old horseshoes to the children, for their games.

My father, who was too shy to speak to anyone, slipped one around her wrist as she browsed. She looked up, startled by the gesture and his boldness, the unexpected weight of the shoe, then the iron, which quickly warmed against her. It startled him, too, because he had never done something like that before.

They didn't see each other again until a few days later, at the same stall, when she returned, her fingers stiff from repeating a phrase on the piano all morning. She had wanted to look at his face one more time. He smelled like hay and fire.

She never returned home. She followed him north and tried to make a life with him in the Hudson Valley, both of them in their twenties, with the barrier of language between them, and only the faith of some attraction they held on to for as long as they could.

Joséphine gave lessons here. They had me.

Then, in 1914, everything changed. She heard about France on the radio. She wanted to do something. I used to think that if she could, she would have gone back. But she didn't. She pulled away from my father instead. I never discovered what caused this or whether they themselves could have articulated it. But they drifted apart, quietly, over time, as I grew older, creating separate lives, separate rhythms to their days.

My father I saw less of. He took on more work in the farms across the valley and came back well into evening. Years later, in those times when I would think of him, it was never his face I recalled but his shape in the distance, in the field, as he went to shoe a horse. Or the way his arm hung over the chair as he fell asleep, the book he was trying to read slipping from his hand and dropping. How I would pick the book up, sit on the floor with his palm on my head, and wait for the twitch of some dream, imagining what world he had found himself in as I listened to his steady breathing.

It was my mother I spent most days with. Helping her around the house. Going into town with her to buy draperies for the windows. *My love, help*, she would say, and I rushed to collect the gauzy fabric that spilled from her arms like old sails. And when she began to volunteer at the sanatorium, she took me, and I watched as, through the years, she helped the patients and later the North American wounded who were sent up from the city, along the river, and transported here by trucks, to be closer to home, to recover, to die.

I outlived her. How was that possible? I never knew what made her, in a slow descent over the years, begin to use the medicine she gave to the patients at the sanatorium. What it was she hid or kept from me and my father.

But I loved being with her then. I loved watching her work. Her patience and charm with strangers. Her uniform, and her dark hair I didn't inherit, pinned up. Up there, she laughed easily. She was gregarious. She sang French songs for the convalescents and for me.

And I loved, almost as much, the sanatorium itself, which was tall and endless, with all its windows and dormers, the heavy curtains and the chandeliers like some old palace. The rocking chairs on the porch, which faced a lake. And Theo, who would come down from the house that was connected to the main building, carrying a towel the size of a bed over his shoulder, to take me swimming.

Theo was the son of the resident physician. They were

British but had come here when he was an infant, their father working first in the city. No one knew where his mother was. They had already been at the sanatorium by the time my mother began to volunteer. Theo and I were around the same age and we often sought each other's company on the mountain, the two of us floating on our backs in the lake, wondering about what was happening in France.

He was smaller than I was, but he moved like a dancer to me. Light-footed and assured as we explored the floors of the building, hunting for ghosts and secret passageways. He liked to show me the patients that terrified him. A man with strange scars across his chest; another who couldn't stop coughing and spitting up blood. He would bend down toward the keyhole, his long bangs falling over his eyes, and peer in.

Eventually, my mother found us, kissed Theo and me, and she and I headed back down before it grew dark. Theo, like a gentleman, always walked us to the start of the trail, watched from there, and waved.

I never saw him leave the mountain. It didn't occur to me to think of that as odd then. He was always Theo on the mountain, as my mother called him. Like she had done for me, she taught him some French. Brought him pastries from the town.

Later, I heard he was sick. An incurable illness. I never found out what it was or if this was true. He was strong to me. Bright-eyed. He dove often and first into the lake. Held his breath the longest. Ran across the lawn the fastest. But one day he didn't appear outside. And I didn't see him the next day either. And when I hadn't seen him in a long time, I was told he had gone away. Him and his father both. No one seemed to know where, not even my mother.

A new physician moved in. The days grew colder. I wrapped myself in a blanket I had stolen from a ward and sat on the rocking chairs with the wounded who had begun to appear from France. One was named Henri Loze, but he went by Henry. He was Canadian. He let me hold his cigarette lighter. He spoke of the Argonne. He joked about the girls in Calais. About the one he met on a bridge who had followed him, trying to sell shoelaces, buttons, bottles, things taken from dead soldiers.

Oh, her breasts, he said, and he began to cry, open-mouthed, his shoulders shaking and his saliva dripping onto his blanket, which hid the fact that he was missing his legs.

My mother appeared and gave him something—I couldn't tell what—and I saw her slip something else under the sleeve of her shirt as Henry called her by her name and, in the warm sunlight, calmed.

II.

My father came up to the sanatorium a few times. He told me this in a letter once, many years later, saying good-bye. He used to watch as Theo and I followed the paths, caught in our own private worlds. And later, when I was older, he watched as I helped some patients into the boat so that they could row out across the lake. He said he liked seeing me in my uniform. He thought my mother would have liked seeing it, too.

He never told me if he ever approached her while she was working or whether he simply stayed for a while at the edge of the property and climbed back down. Whether he ever continued on to the building and talked to anyone, curious about the place that perhaps still contained some part of my childhood and that had consumed his wife so deeply. He never told me if he ever found her in the corner of a room, erasing herself with the morphine she had continued to use and that, one day, she never woke from.

Two orderlies found her. And then they came down, meeting my father in the field beside our house and, in a moment of grief I wasn't witness to, he beat them, nearly killing one.

My father left not long after. I didn't know where he went. Just that he walked to the docks one night, got on a boat, and left the valley, his house, and the horses he had worked with all his life.

I never saw him again. It was the start of the Second World War and I used to wonder if, like me, he had entered it somewhere, in some far continent. For a time, I checked lists and asked people passing through if they had seen him, or knew him, but no one ever did.

I was in England during those years. I had joined the Red Cross, working for a hospital in London. I was almost thirty, unmarried, and I spent most days in the wards, doing what my mother had done, or wandering the streets, not yet accustomed to the city. There was a café near the hospital and from my window at night I would listen to faint music, sometimes a singer. I tried to name the café songs. I read again the only letter my father ever wrote to me, surprised that he had written at all, surprised that it arrived:

The sanatorium closed. I think because of the war. Like you,
all the doctors have gone. Tomorrow I will go up to the garden
they were growing and take what is left of the vegetables. I
am here in the room with the piano, noticing for the first time
that it is missing a key. Was it always missing? Yesterday, I had
a dream of you as a boy: I was in a chair and you were sitting
on the floor beside me, leaning up into my hand.

*   *   *

The bombings started that fall. I disobeyed orders and stayed, living in the hospital basement for one hundred fifty days.

More than anything, we cherished lightbulbs.

Once, in a narrow corridor, a girl asked for my address. She had given me hers, slipped it into my shirt pocket.

In case, she said.

I didn't have time to give her mine. I hadn't even caught her name. She had reached for my shoulder, touched me as though playing a game. It was the lightest touch. Her eyes delirious in the dust and the blinking dark as she rushed by, pushing a wounded man against the wall to steady him, to operate on him.

I took out the paper. An address in Montreal.

I thought I saw her again during those one hundred fifty days. There was a six-inch window in the room I shared with seven others as we took turns trying to sleep. It was our only view out into a city that was being destroyed, hour by hour. We watched families attempt to scavenge whatever they could—a cup, a radio, a window curtain—as the cobblestone around them was pummeled. I saw the branch of a tree fly into the air and spear a woman's heart, catapulting her backward into a crater.

Paper fell like snow.

Across the courtyard, there was another window, where there were other doctors and nurses. The passage connecting the wings of the hospital had long ago collapsed, so we signaled to each other with candles, this brief joy at catching the blurred, lit shapes of other people's faces over the rubble.

I thought I saw her there, her profile passing the windowpane. I waved. In a moment of quiet someone lifted her and she squeezed through the window and I watched her sprint, waving a flashlight. I wondered if she was looking for something or going to find help or running away. The light hit my eyes and I lost her.

That night the statue in the courtyard fell and covered our window. We lost electricity. For the rest of the days we were strict with our candles in that room that smelled of our bodies and the earth. Ten minutes every evening to see each other and remind ourselves we were still there, and to write our letters. We had a gramophone and one undamaged record, Billie Holiday, so we listened to a song as we wrote.

I didn't know who to write to, so I wrote every night to Theo:

1940–1941

Canada. I like the sound of that word in my mouth. It feels like a calm winter to me. A warm fire. A word to hold. Maybe my father's there. Maybe you are, too. One day I'll visit. I'll knock on your door with the pastries you love, the ones with the chocolate in the center.

I want to see the landscape we tried to paint together—you started with twilight; I put in a harbor and a small boat. Was it cruel to paint alongside the patients? I wonder. The ones who painted to pass the hours, to distract themselves from death. You never met Henry Loze. You would have liked him. He was funny and kind and told stories. He often held himself as though trying to vanish.

I am starting to understand that instinct, when wounded, to find a small, dark space. Through the only window I see a narrow strip of sky and I wonder if that is enough. I am beginning to grow comfortable here in the dark. I am beginning to get used to the air. I wonder if I will ever step outside again. Maybe I was always here.

I think we live in museums.

There were once photographs on the walls of this building. Portraits. The faces of the first doctors. The countryside in the evening. A lake, low-lit. A willow and the moon. We burned them for fire.

I keep thinking of your laughter. Which was like the snow. A note on the piano. The shape of air. We promised each other we would never steal from the pockets of the dead. I broke that promise here.

I'm losing track of time.

Once in a fit of anger I broke off a key from my mother's piano and hid it in the sanatorium's attic. It must still be there. My mother never scolded me, even though she knew I was the one who had done it. She continued to play, masking that missing note.

Theo, you first stole the morphine for her, didn't you? You thought it was a game. You would sneak into your father's office, unlock the cabinets, and come back to her, waiting for her to smile, waiting to feel her hand on your hair. I knew. But I'm not angry about that. I think you knew you were dying. And you did everything you could to please everyone. You, who would never come down from that mountain. Only wave. As though there was something in your life, something deep and bright, that was never in mine.

I saw you once leap into a rainstorm like an animal, like a swimmer, your wild body lit by lightning.

I have come to think privacy is both sacred and sacrilege.

Tonight, I don't remember my father. I look up at the window where a stone face, with a shattered eye, stares down.

III.

It ended in the spring. I didn't leave right away. We found as many people as we could, or they found us, and we treated them. We swept, we cleaned. We repaired walls and windows. And then in the summer, as I was leaving the hospital on an errand, a family followed me out. Two children and their parents. They appeared dazed in the heat and the sun, unsure of where they were, what day it was, what year. They stayed close to me and didn't speak.

I was supposed to pick up medicine from a mill that had been converted into a barracks. Instead, I took the children's hands and helped them over the rubble and around the wagons and the wheelbarrows.

We saw the Thames. We followed the curve of the river, past town homes and factories with tall smokestacks. In what had been a store, three mannequins stood unharmed, their clothes gone, and the children stopped to mimic their poses. A café was open, serving coffee, and the father bought one and shared it with his wife, the two of them taking turns holding the ceramic cup. It was hotter now in the afternoon, and I had nothing, only my uniform.

As the day went on I thought I recognized the father. I thought he had been in the basement room with me. I didn't remember a family. The woman was wearing boots like the ones soldiers wore. There were holes in the leather and as she stepped over mounds of bricks and cobblestone I could see flashes of her orange-colored socks.

We kept walking. No one bothered us. We reached a hill as the sun went down. In the distance, small fires were beginning to form; they were on the streets, along the river, in houses that were missing walls and roofs. We could see people gather, lift their hands for warmth. I thought I heard a gunshot. The echo. Glass breaking. I could see the mill I was supposed to have gone to, standing on the outskirts of the city near a long field. I spotted someone in a wheelchair navigating a blocked bridge. An old woman bent down on a street to water a flower that was still alive.

It was getting late. We were hungry and tired. The children wandered the ridge as though at a loss, confused as to how they ended up here in the growing dark, so far away. The father turned to me wanting to know what I would do, what they should all do, and I did nothing.

I missed my mother. I missed what little I ever had of my father. In that moment, on that ridge, I imagined the days before they met. And that whatever labyrinth they had run into when they were young had never happened. That he continued to sell horseshoes at a city market, and she was playing the piano in the evening, in an auditorium. And that I was there. Now. In the audience, watching as the braid of her hair came loose and fell with the notes, under the lights.

That night we caught a supply train heading north, and as we left the city, the family fell asleep in the corner of the car, huddled together with their arms around each other. I cracked open the door. I watched as we entered the country, unable to remember the last time I saw a living tree.

Hours later, I felt the shock of the ocean ahead of me— the bright expanse of it, the glass.

I lost the family. When morning came they left, jumping off into a high grass meadow where there were horses, and entered their new life.

I kept going. I wasn't yet used to being alone.

Eventually, the train stopped at a depot somewhere in the late night, and I snuck away into the country. I followed the moon. I found a tall maple where I sat down and, for the first time, wept.

IV.

Years later, I returned to the sanatorium.

I walked from the town. I started early in the morning, following the trail up the mountain. It was the end of summer. It was beautiful to see the valley and the colors and the fog that was moving over everything.

I wasn't sure what to expect. I thought someone would be there. Some old hope. But I found it still abandoned. Windowpanes were broken and the paint of the structure had peeled away long ago. There were three rocking chairs left on the rotting porch. They were close together, facing the lake, which held the reflection of clouds, the water breaking from a bird. In the courtyard, a bicycle wheel was lying in the fountain. I could smell the wet, undisturbed earth.

The entrance doors seemed the only thing that looked as how I remembered them: ancient, mythical. Doors for giants. I pushed and, to my surprise, they opened, creaking loudly, a burst of stale, cold air escaping. From a hole in the high ceiling, feathers fell down the height of four stories, past the bones of a chandelier.

I wandered the halls. In the rooms, some of the cots were still made with clean linen; others had old evidence of squatters. There were clothes in drawers, crosses on the walls. I found a spinning top, like the one I used to have as a child. Daguerreotypes of people I didn't recognize. The sun came through the windows, reflecting off the metal trays on the tables. The cabinets were empty, all the drugs and medicine gone.

I ended up on the top floor, where the ceiling followed the shape of the mansard roof. I liked that floor best when I was a child, with its strange angles and the rows of beds like some orphanage in a story. It would grow unbearably hot and no one actually slept up there in the summers, so it was ours, I thought, mine and Theo's, some private place we claimed.

Through the dormer windows there was a view below of the house where Theo and his father used to live. The grounds surrounding the house still looked as they had when I was young, and I was happy. I had survived the war. I was here.

I leaned down. I lifted the loose plank under one of the beds. I reached in.

My fingers caught something cold, and I pulled it back up and held it to the light. My mother's piano key, worn from the years and her playing, which I pocketed before I went outside.

*   *   *

I still thought of it as Theo's house, though of course it hadn't been for a very long time. None of his things, or his father's things, were there anymore but there was a bed, a long table in the kitchen, framed maps on the walls, and some books on the shelves—things I assumed had belonged to the other physicians who had lived here after.

Mice had nibbled at the large rug on the floor. I dragged it to the porch and beat the dust from it. I swept the floor. I straightened the maps on the walls. I had brought some food with me from the town—a loaf of bread, sardine tins, cheese, tomatoes—it was plenty for a few days.

I wondered who had stayed here through the years. I flipped through the books. Some of them fell apart in my hands, and I collected the pages and tucked them in again. I had planned on visiting my own house, but the hours passed. I pulled the sheets from a convalescent's room and came back and made the bed.

That night I slept in Theo's house for the first time, thinking I would begin in the main building tomorrow, collect the broken glass and the trays, fix the rocking chairs. I dreamed of Theo's father. We were in London together in an empty factory without walls. He was wearing his doctor's coat and giving me a tour. In his arms, he was carrying lightbulbs, and

I knew they were for the chandelier. Then something far in the city collapsed, and I opened my eyes.

One day, a young woman and a boy appeared on the mountain. I hadn't seen them come up. They were standing on the lawn, holding hands and looking out at the open valley. I wondered if they were lost. It was late in the afternoon. The woman was wearing a long-brimmed hat and carrying a long canister of some kind. She was perhaps in her twenties. The boy was about five. I watched from the door as they crossed over to the lake. Leaves had begun to fall into the water. She let the boy walk over to the small dock, beside the rowboat, and he studied his reflection.

The woman saw me and waved, so I made my way out to her. The other day, scraping the walls, I had fallen off the ladder and wrenched my knee. It was better now but I was moving a bit slowly and she met me halfway.

We shook hands. She introduced herself as Elsa Marie Loze and I immediately recognized the family name. She was Henry's daughter. She had been on a trip, on her way back to Montreal, when she remembered her father had been a patient here.

She looked around and behind me at the building.

And this is Tom, she said.

Hi, Tom, I said, and the boy buried his head against his mother's legs.

Do you live here? Elsa Marie said.

Just for a little while, I said.

Like a caretaker? she said.

Yes, I said. Something like that.

Shadows had begun to extend across the lawn. I could hear a wind passing through the high leaves. She opened the canister she had been carrying.

He became a painter, you know, she said. My father. A decent one. A museum was interested in his work, so I brought some down with me. Here. Come look.

We went to the car and carried the rest to the house. She rolled them out for me on the kitchen table. I made her tea while Tom explored, studying the maps on the walls and playing with the spinning top I had found. He fell asleep in the chair by the fire, holding an opened book and wearing his mother's hat.

The paintings were mostly of Montreal. The quays and the water in winter. A pastry shop on rue Saint-Jacques. A pair of children's boots over a telephone wire. Others he had done from memory. The mountain lake. The two children from a theater troupe who had appeared at the sanatorium one summer—they had gotten lost, showing up on the mountain in the evening in their costumes, like a dream, the girl with her face painted and the boy with wings.

I stopped at a portrait of a young girl in a concert hall, playing the piano.

That is Joséphine Belgard, she said.

I didn't respond. I waited to see if she would say anything more. I stared at the painting, not wanting to ever look up.

Here was something I learned that day: Henry Loze knew who she was. He had always known. When he was younger his parents had taken him to see her perform. She had gone to Canada before heading to New York. She was going to be a star. The next Chopin. Hands like birds. Hands that would, a lifetime later, lift him into a bathtub on his first day here and wash his body.

What made someone give up a life and start another? What made my mother stay in New York? What did she think she was stepping toward? She chose my father and the shape of a life she could have never imagined. For many years I was sure she regretted it. But perhaps this was untrue.

The light in the room was falling. Elsa Marie checked her watch and said that she had to go, that she should get on the road. She asked if there was a restaurant in the town.

I said there was. I asked where she was staying.

Staying? she said, looking across at the boy. We're driving. Canada, tonight.

She said Tom loved the road.

We've been all over, she said. Just him and me. My one, true man.

She bent down, lifted her hat, and picked him up so that his head rested on her shoulder, and she carried him like that as I opened the door. I brought her hat and the paintings for her. We made our way to the front of the main building where she had parked.

I want to ask you something, she said. Before we go. Do you know which room was Henry's?

Yes, I said, and pointed to a window on the first floor, facing the lake.

The sun was now moving behind the ridge. She climbed up to the porch. Carefully, with the boy still asleep on her, she peered through the broken window.

You were in the war? she said.

I said I was.

She pointed at my knee and said, Will you be all right?

I will be all right, I said.

She stood back up. But then, changing her mind, she sat down on one of the rocking chairs, still carrying Tom.

Maybe I'll rest for a moment, she said, and sighed.

She looked tired. I could see the fatigue in the way she carried the boy or maybe it was something else I couldn't articulate. She looked lovely, sitting there against the last of the daylight, and I wondered where she had been and what her years had been like.

I wondered when Henry died. What he was like as a father. Where all our time had gone.

It was getting cold. I gave her my coat, which she draped over the two of them, and she rocked once, in the chair, and settled. So I sat with her.

Look at that, she said.

She had turned toward the lake. The rowboat had become untethered and was now drifting away. I saw it move as though it were being pulled by a long string, going farther and fading.

I watched until I couldn't see it anymore.

Then Elsa Marie, holding her boy, closed her eyes, and the day ended, and there was only the water in the night.

STILL A FIRE

Mikel, 1947–48

He waits with the others.

He finds a small space on the already crowded bench that faces the river and when there is the sound of an engine he turns and focuses on the distant headlights or the dust rising from the dirt road. Otherwise he watches the tugboats pulling shipping containers toward the Calais harbor while some of the men shout at the pilots, asking if they are hiring. They blow into their hands. They pace. They throw pebbles at the ships, though no one ever throws far enough to hit them.

Once, a sailor came out, spun a few times on the deck, and launched a small package in their direction. It was the size of a grenade and one of the men had reached for Mikel's hand, terrified as it landed on the lower bank. Mikel let go and went to retrieve it. It was a pack of cigarettes with a note wrapped around it telling them to *go fuck themselves*. They smoked the pack that day.

Mikel is the youngest of them. Twenty-four. He also stays the longest. If no one comes the older ones give up and return to the shantytown. A few of them move on, following the river toward the city, hoping to find work there or on the way. There is a new automobile factory down the road and sometimes it is possible to find a temporary job there, working a line or mopping the floors after hours.

In the past two years Mikel has worked for farms regrowing flowers and grains and for companies hired to sift through the rubble of what had been city blocks. He has carried boxes and furniture for the families returning to their homes or moving somewhere else. He has even carried their children, the parents too tired to lift anything. Sometimes a man drives up to the bench and wants company, and Mikel watches as one or two shrug, agree on a price, open the door, and go in.

What wouldn't he do? In the night, distracted by hunger and unable to sleep, he makes a list, or tries to. It seems important to him, to try to know what he wouldn't do. He thinks he is the kind of person who would enter the car of a man and keep him company. He never does but perhaps he will one day. He thinks this, turns over, and holds his breath as though he wants to swallow the thought.

It was the dogs he couldn't stomach. When he collected rubble in the city blocks. He will all his life think of them, the dogs. The starving ones that had entered a pile for shelter. Too weak to move as the workers picked them up with the debris and bricks and threw the animals away into the trucks.

That day Mikel collapsed and vomited. Perhaps he blacked out, he wasn't sure, only that the workers left him there and moved on. When he looked up he was alone. He was beside a broken wall where someone had painted a tree with lipstick.

He waits until the evening and then he walks home. He is with his neighbor Artur, a Romanian, and they follow the river west away from the city and toward the mountains. It is growing dark but there are still the bright lights of the factories across the water, bright enough to illuminate this side of the bank. Three stars have appeared, above. They stumble upon an American C-ration can on the dirt road. Artur picks it up, shakes it beside his ear. They are still sold on the black market and there are a few crumbs of a biscuit left on the bottom. Artur licks his finger and presses down. He offers half of the remaining crumbs to Mikel.

Mikel regrets it at once because he grows aware of his hunger. He knows Artur feels this, too, because he crushes the can and kicks it toward Mikel. So they begin kicking the can back and forth to distract themselves as they walk. When a car passes they pick it up and hide it as though it were something valuable. Then they try to wave the car down for a ride, though no one ever stops. Still they try every time, the headlights sweeping over their bodies.

They keep walking and playing. Artur balances the can on his foot before shooting it back over. But Mikel misses, and Artur raises his arms and runs briefly in a circle. Mikel retrieves the can and chases him. It feels good to keep moving like this in the cold as it grows darker.

When they catch their breaths, Artur says, I think they're testing.

They are talking about the explosion they heard earlier that day. Or the faint trail of it. A few claps of thunder from somewhere in the mountains. Though they knew enough to know it wasn't thunder.

Testing for what? Mikel says.

For the next one, Artur says. The next conflict. To be better.

Mikel kicks the can back. He thinks it's from the miners. They resumed coal mining farther south and some of the men have gotten steady work there, moving to the temporary cabins that have been built for them, bringing their families if they have families. He envies them, envies the solidness of their days. He envies their families.

Artur is younger than he is. He speaks with a heavy accent. In a year he has discovered little about him. It is how they all live in the shantytown. They know only a few facts about each other. It isn't conscious; it is, he thinks, a resigned exhaustion after the years that have gone. They survived. What else is there to say? There is little they want to talk about that doesn't have to do with today. They don't even want to talk about tomorrow.

He knows Artur was infantry and that he has a younger brother and that the brother is sick. Artur works to support both of them.

There were days in the past year Mikel has told a perspective employer to hire Artur instead, walking away and returning to the bench. And he is uncertain if that is something he should be doing when it is difficult to find work every day, and he is uncertain whether Artur at all cares. But they are the only people in Mikel's life, so he does it anyway.

They are approaching the shantytown now. In the dark

they can make out the bare lightbulbs strung up in the shacks and along the eaves of the tin roofs. The bulbs create severe shadows everywhere, a person's silhouette drifting like a ghost along the paths. Artur picks up the crushed can and they enter the field, smelling food being boiled, hearing dogs and the noise of a radio over the hum of the power generator.

Artur's brother is in the distance, sweeping litter with a broom. They know it is him because he is the tallest of them and the one with the poorest posture. Emil cannot work but he does what he can among the shanties, helping anyone who needs it.

Though Artur has never confirmed this, there is a rumor that in Romania, Emil had been a painter. Perhaps it isn't true. Perhaps the rumor started because he collects canisters of paint from the nearby landfill in the valley.

In France, building-repair projects have created a wealth of discarded paint. So there are days when Emil appears on the paths, pushing a cart with a pyramid of tin canisters. If an occupant wants him to, Emil will paint their shacks in whatever color he found. He has painted over a dozen shacks already, some in stripes, some in solids or geometric patterns, so that during the day there are bright shapes scattered in the long field.

Emil waves as they approach and they join him outside

where there is a bench he has made out of wood planks and empty paint canisters. None of them have brought back food tonight. Or money. But they have tea and the stale pastries Artur found the other day in the city, watching a baker throw away everything he didn't sell. Thinking this insane, Artur took as much as he could, stuffing bread and pastries into his pockets, in his excitement forgetting that some were filled with cream and fruit. They burst on his way home, ruining his clothes.

How much Emil had laughed. Mikel, too, when he heard.

They eat what is left and laugh again and even in the cold they remain outside, talking about the day.

Artur's brother seems both aware of Mikel's presence and unaware of him. Mikel has never heard the man speak. Emil is a giant who can vanish at any moment, whenever he wishes. On occasion he brushes some dirt off of Artur's shoulder or looks out into the lighted evening at the flicker of a bat. A dog appears, chasing a rodent or following the scent of food. When the dog finds its way to them Emil leans forward and feeds it the leftover bread.

Mikel wonders what illness the brother has. He knows it is something in the head. There are days when Emil never goes outside. Other days when all he does is stay outside, heading to the landfill. He has watched Emil help others but he has also watched him swing a piece of wood at people he doesn't know, people who aren't from here scavenging—swung and lunged at them in a way that made Mikel stop from approaching him.

It is odd that the brothers' own shanty hasn't been painted. It is bare, just the colors of the wood and the metal they have found for it. As though some personal seed of belief has escaped Emil. He can do what someone else wants but he can't do the same for himself. Or perhaps he doesn't know what he himself wants. Perhaps he wouldn't know what to paint. Mikel understands that.

Did you hear the explosion? Artur says.

His brother doesn't answer.

Testing, Artur says, his mouth full of bread.

Mikel imagines the life Emil once had. What his days were like. What kind of paintings he did. Whether there are paintings of his somewhere on a wall or in a vault or buried in a pile of other things forgotten. Or whether they were discarded or burned. He wonders if he will ever see one. He wonders what it means for someone to be a painter. What it takes for someone to stop doing the thing he has always done.

Mikel has done nothing special. This doesn't bother him. He doesn't know if it should. It was a life. He moved with his parents. He harvested flowers with them. Worked the Basque farms. He was good at finding things his mother misplaced. A mirror. A brush. As a child he knelt by the river once, pointed, thought he had found the actual moon.

Mikel is tired. He has done nothing today and yet he is tired. He watches as the brothers rest their heads against each other, grateful to be together again. The sudden physical intimacy tears something in Mikel. He looks down the path. He catches the dog moving in between shacks. The clatter of beads someone has hung outside their entrance. Calais in the distance and the curve of the moon. Briefly the smell of the coast. He never imagined he would live in northern France.

He thanks them for the food and stands. Artur whistles as he leaves. Mikel turns, glimpsing the crushed can in the air, and reaches out to catch it.

Good night, Mikel says. See you tomorrow, good night.

His shanty stands farther down the path. It has been painted blue, a blue that he cannot see in the evening. He lifts aside the wood plank he has been using for a door. There is very little inside. There are a few blankets, a deck of playing cards he had gotten from a tinker, when his parents had stopped to help the man fix a wheel. He had told his parents to pick whatever they wanted and they had let Mikel choose.

He could have picked something useful to them—a pan, a ball of thread, winter socks—but he picked the cards. He had never seen their design before. They were from Germany. Some missionaries had brought them. The tinker didn't know more than that, didn't know if they were called anything different or what kind of games you played with them.

In the shanty he lies down and opens the frayed case that still carries the cards. He looks at the illustrations of the drummers and the knights. He counts the cards knowing he is missing one, has been missing one for many years. He tries to make his list again of all the things he wouldn't do. He listens to the people still awake in the shantytown. Someone's radio.

He should have picked something useful. When the tinker had asked. But he picked these cards and his parents didn't mind. Didn't mind even when they could have used those winter socks. They brought the cards wherever they went and invented their own games and rules of play. *The Flying Horseshoe. The King of the Woods. The Divine Palace. The Horse and the Moon.* They played when they could, the three of them.

One evening on a flower farm in the southern French mountains he woke to find his parents had fallen asleep together sitting against the trunk of a tree. It was summer and beautiful and they had been delaying heading inside. Above them on a low branch hung a wind chime. His parents' heads were bowed and their hands were trembling as though they were still picking flowers together. As though they were conversing in their dreams.

These two people in his life who could be as private as a tunnel.

They had been playing cards. Some had slipped from their fingers and scattered. So Mikel walked the field, looking for as many as he could in the grass. The wind chime clattered. He kept the melody in his periphery as he searched. He never found them all. When he returned he sat down near them, to be with them, and his father stirred. He knew it was him, not his mother. But Mikel didn't turn. He didn't know why but he didn't turn. He stayed facing the farm and his father moved over to him, lay down, pressed his head in the space between Mikel's shoulders, and fell back asleep there.

He thought of how his father never did this again. Of the soft weight of his father on his back. He thought he would like to find that farm again. That field of flowers. That constant melody in the night air. Was it a fragment of a song?

Mikel catches music coming from a distant shanty. Someone passes his door. And then someone else. Like the shadows of a carousel. And then there is nothing, only the spaces in the walls where the moonlight enters.

•

The next day a truck pulls up to the spot. It is an old military pickup truck though it could be anyone. In Calais they are everywhere, the abandoned American and British automobiles that civilians took for themselves. They are in the streets downtown, in the fields, along the river where Mikel is. They are painted over if paint is available or they are covered with tape or anything else, their disguise so crude and makeshift at times you wonder why they cover the markings at all. No one cares.

On this truck, *Sunshine Clearance* is written on a piece of cardboard glued to the side of the door.

There are only five on the bench. It is just before dawn and not everyone has arrived. But they all stand and approach. They haven't seen the two men already on the flatbed. They were lying down, napping, but get up now to look around, their eyes taking in the river as though they have never seen it.

Then a man rolls down the passenger-side window and points at Artur, who is the youngest.

Can you walk? the man says.

He doesn't understand the question.

Of course I can walk, Artur says.

Distances. Slopes. Higher altitude. Good lungs?

Artur flicks the cigarette he was smoking onto the road.

Great, he says.

The man seems to consider him. His accent.

Russian?

Romanian.

Jew?

Fuck if you care, Artur says, growing impatient.

The man laughs. He looks over at the others. None of them can tell whom he is looking at because the man is wearing sunglasses. He is older and keeps the truck running.

Today, you work until dark. But only half-day pay. Then if all goes okay you start again at dawn tomorrow. Full-day pay.

Okay, Artur says.

He reaches for the door but the man tells him to get in the back. The man studies the four remaining and points at Mikel.

You, too.

Mikel climbs in. The remaining three return to the bench and watch them go. They speed north along the river road and as they near the shantytown they pass the other men heading toward the bench. They recognize each other and

37

wave. On the river a fishing vessel moves in the opposite direction. The moon is still out. The other two on the flatbed have gone back to sleep. Mikel smells wet leaves and urine. He helps Artur light a cigarette in the wind, both of them aware that the man never said what the work is. Then they are gone, past the shanties, farther into the countryside toward the mountains.

The day is starting and as the fog pulls away he sees more of the ruined landscape, the peaks and the bare slopes where trees have yet to grow again. He pulls up the collars of his coat as the wind grows louder. Artur doesn't mind the wind. He leans back and shuts his eyes as though it is still summer.

The truck turns onto a steep mountain road. The flatbed shakes and a metal tube slides out from underneath the tarp between them. Mikel lifts the corner but catches the man looking at them from the rearview. He recognizes what the tube is but doesn't think of why it is there. He looks across at Artur and the other men but they all have their eyes closed, luxuriating now in the sudden morning light. For the first time he studies the faces of the two but he has never seen them before. They have beards and they dip their heads over the edge of the truck, exposing their pale throats.

They enter a forest. The road narrows as they continue

to climb. It grows dim again and then bright. They turn once more and follow a road that has the track marks of a tank still caked into the dirt. Someone has dropped sandbags to cover the holes in the road. A sign appears in both French and English but he doesn't catch it. They pass another one. Two more. Now Mikel reads them. He leans over. So does Artur. They have yet to speak. They look at each other and then at the tarp by their feet and it is as though they are asking the other what to do but not knowing how.

Up ahead, a tall mound of stones is blocking the road. The truck stops and the man tells them to pick up what is under the tarp and follow him. Mikel doesn't have a watch but perhaps it has taken two hours to get here. The light is different here, in this forest. The tall trees severing daylight.

As Artur lifts the tarp, Mikel looks back at the tank treads, something he hasn't seen in a year. They are like fossils, the spines of dinosaurs. He thinks of the men he has seen over the years, sweeping the roads. There are six of them on the flatbed: metal detectors the Army had once used, old now, the grips frayed, the radios scratched up.

He looks across the truck but the man with sunglasses and the other two have already vanished over the stone pile. He hears the man's voice and he decides in that moment that he will run. He wants to but the man returns, showing them their payment and tells them to hurry. Artur jumps down. Artur doesn't run. He climbs over the stones and then Mikel climbs, too, carrying two of the detectors and the radios, which are in canvas bags slung over his shoulder. There is a log just beyond, blocking the road again, and they are all waiting for him there.

As Mikel approaches, he asks the man what the sign on the truck door means. *Sunshine Clearance*. He doesn't understand.

I think it's funny, their new employer says, and takes a detector and a radio. We clear with a smile.

The man smiles with great exaggeration.

He tells them not to lift the coil but to keep it parallel to the ground. He shows them what sound they make through the radio, dropping a few nails and sweeping over them. He says all this very quickly and Mikel can tell Artur doesn't understand everything. The man checks his watch and tosses them a bottle of talcum powder for their hands. The man is waiting for them to head in.

Mikel knows now what happened to the tank. They can see it over the log farther down the forest road, under the bowing trees, emptied of itself and broken. Blood splatter is crusted on its shell, though he convinces himself it probably isn't, that it is mud. A wind comes again. He thinks of the money and wants to step in but his body is unable to. His mouth has dried up. He holds his breath. The talcum feels like pinpricks on his fingertips. He understands what the sound was that he heard yesterday. He searches for a fresh crater. He cannot find it.

Artur waits beside him. Mikel knows what they are about to do and he wants to go back to the bench on the river. To sit with the others. He wants this day to end. To walk back to his shanty. To start again tomorrow. He will find something else. He always has. He thinks if Artur ran right now he would, too. He thinks this, gripping the detector as a shadow traces the road. An airplane flies overhead.

It's simple, the man says, his voice softer and slower, as though he has done this many times before. They are only there to sweep and detect. That is all. Another team will come in for removal and clearance. He says words like this in a way that makes Mikel wonder if the man is a veteran, too.

He will never see him again after today. He will never know a single thing about this man except he is the kind of person who thinks the words on his truck door are funny. Mikel doesn't yet know that there is a market for undetonated mines in these years after the war. That there is a market for any weapon anyone can find. That you can make more money doing this than you ever had in your life.

Years from now and far from here, Mikel will try to re-call if he understood the insanity of the man who brought them to this forest. If he thought of this at all as they began to move across the two-kilometer road that was once used by loggers and miners and then later the Germans. If Mikel understood, it meant he didn't care. Or it didn't matter enough.

Artur doesn't run. Artur mutters a Romanian word and steps over the log first. Artur begins to sweep and the oth-ers follow. Mikel is the last to go. He still doesn't believe he will even as he watches Artur move down the road, hears the man behind him say, Go.

So Mikel steps in. He is over the log now. Past the signs. He takes another step and sweeps. He hears nothing. He has forgotten to turn the radio on. He stops to make sure it is buzzing and sweeps again, suddenly grateful for the powder that absorbs the moisture that has begun to seep from his palms.

Another airplane flies overhead. The sound of it is shat-tering. It hooks his rib from the inside as though he is a fish and yanks. His legs clatter. The wind is so cold. He wants to scream. He thinks he will feel better if he screams. Perhaps in the momentary noise he does.

He keeps track of Artur as though tethered to him.

They are across from each other on the road, following the ditches. The others from the truck have already moved ahead of them. They have all been assigned areas, arbitrary distances the man decided on by pointing to a branch of a tree where the leaves have turned mustard colored. They are to start at the perimeter along the ditches and then circle in toward the center.

Where has the man gone? He is perhaps behind them, waiting by the log. Mikel doesn't turn. He looks down at his feet. At legs he believed were shaking but are still. As he moves forward he isn't convinced he is sweeping but he is, he can see the coil gliding over the dirt and the grass. His own powdered fist. He passes an empty glass bottle in a ditch. A cluster of wildflowers. Then: the reflection of a small, bright object. He doesn't wonder what it is. He thinks of a wristwatch his father used to wear. He wore it loose and Mikel would slip his fingers under the band whenever they walked together or slept in the freight car of a train as they traveled from one farm to another. The wristband was how his father taught him how to skate. They used to skate rivers in the winter, in the late night as people lit fires on the banks for them to see. The blue ice, their blue breaths, his fingers tucked under his father's wristwatch as they glided.

He thinks of rivers as he tracks Artur. Then trains. He

would like to travel again. Perhaps it is time to move on, to somewhere else, wherever that may be. They never had a home. Home was a cart and two horses.

He concentrates on the rhythm of the sweeping. He listens to the frequency of the radio and keeps going. He thinks only of the sweeping and the frequency. His breathing. The heavy sweeping. His palms begin to sweat. He calls for more talcum powder but the man doesn't respond. He grips the handle harder and takes another step and another. Now he hears nothing in the cavern of the forest road. Nothing but his breathing.

Artur and the man up ahead move along the perimeter toward the abandoned tank that is perhaps a year old, or older. Then Mikel sees the fresh crater. It is just beyond the tank: a pocket of dark, speckled earth. Artur sees it, too. And then Artur begins to cry. Mikel can hear him over the radio frequency. He can see Artur's twisted face and sees that he is looking down the ditch on his side at something Mikel cannot make out.

What is it? Mikel calls.

The man up ahead stops and looks, too, though he keeps silent. Mikel doesn't know what to do. He doesn't want to stop. He is afraid that if he does he will drop the equipment or fall or step out of the line he has been following. He keeps

walking. He keeps walking and sweeping and he keeps looking at his feet. He leaves behind Artur, who is still crying,
and he keeps moving. He thinks if he moves far enough away
he will be back on the bench and this day will end. He hears
Artur say, I don't want to do this anymore.

Farther in the distance there is a short, muted pop and
its long echo as the dirt of the forest road rises into the air,
dimming the sky with particles of color. It is like a swarm of
bees. It happens before he understands someone was standing there. That whoever it was has vanished.

As he turns back toward Artur, who is still by that ditch,
he sees another man drop his detector. And he hears shouting. And cursing. And then someone appears on the road,
running, as he hears a new noise approaching him, covers his
eyes, and feels, briefly, the sudden sway of trees.

•

Snowdrift has accumulated outside the hospital. New slopes
have formed on the lawn. From the window Mikel watches
an old woman take a tin tray and slide down a shallow hill,
her legs in the air. She tumbles and rolls. Her gray hair un-
ravels in the snow.

He tries to place her among all the people who work
here but she is too far and hidden by the collar of her coat.

She lies there looking up, and Mikel follows her eyes. He sees nothing. Only the flat evenness of a thousand clouds.

It is winter. January. He has watched the year pass learning how to walk again. Three months. Unaware of snow. Unaware of where he is. On this hill overlooking Calais and the sea. He wheeled himself out one day and stopped at the main doors, stunned by the height and the view. Construction cranes. The harbor. Ships and ferries sailing to and from England. He turned back in, not yet used to pushing himself with one hand.

He has stayed away from the front doors since then. He keeps to the long ward, the curtains of privacy. The old bareness. The occasional sound of the old woman passing the window, sledding.

He likes being alone. He tries to be alone here whenever he can. He wheels himself down the corridors and the other wings, exploring a building that survived shelling and mortar rounds seven years ago. All the dents in the walls. Strange mounds of powder that he thinks at first is snow only to see it is the dust of broken stones that have fallen. Windows are still waiting to be replaced. After the building was overrun it had turned into an outpost of some kind, because of its location on the hill. There are old German military maps on a shelf in an office with troop positions. He loves their intricacy: the draftsmanship and the detailed topography. He leans in, trying to remember if he was ever in one of those locations.

One day he forgets that Karine is with him when he folds a few and tucks them under his lap. She takes the maps from him and he thinks she has confiscated them. But when she returns him to his bed, Karine slips the maps beneath his mattress.

How little space she takes. He never notices her there until she is. He never hears her or feels the bed shift.

Karine is the volunteer who has been taking care of him. The hospital has run out of uniforms, so she wears an International Red Cross armband. Mikel knows nothing about her. Only that she visits him every morning and keeps him company. In those early months he keeps staring at her hands.

He lifts his arm that is missing a hand and thinks he survived five years of a war with only the graze of a bullet across his shoulder. He thinks about whether his hand is still there somewhere on that mountain road, buried, or scavenged by birds. He can still feel the fingers, catches them touching his thigh in a dream.

He keeps hearing a wind chime.

When the pain becomes unbearable in his hips and his

back Karine punches him with morphine. And then, check-ing to make sure no one is looking, she inserts the needle into her own arm.

She presses her finger to her lips.

Our secret, Karine says.

He discovers later that she is from the Belgian border. That she is twenty-seven, a few years older than him, and has been working in ICRC hospitals for the past year. She mends tears in her clothes with sutures. Some days she wears lipstick. She always smells of the harbor.

You must try, she always says, helping him into the wheelchair and then, as the months go on, helping him with the crutch.

She walks with him. She talks. Even if he doesn't. He wants to be alone but there is an ease to her he feels himself gravitating toward. This exhausted nurse who has become his one line to the outside.

She talks about the winter and Calais. The new factories. Someone who keeps stealing the flowers in the garden. The lipstick she confesses she steals from a lady in the market. She shows him roof tiles no one can identify, so they keep them in a pile in a room. She shows him the maps. His legs tire and she holds him up and brings him into a room where there is a piano. She settles him onto the bench. She reaches over him and plays a scale, a melody.

Ah! It wasn't a wind chime. It was you.

She looks at him, confused. His first laughter.

One night he wakes to find his blanket disturbed and he thinks it was Karine. But when she appears she tells him someone came to visit him today. He doesn't understand. He is in a lake of morphine, afloat.

A man, Karine says. I don't know his name. Very tall. Mute? He didn't speak. He sat for a while and left.

When the morphine leaves him, even in his pain, he limps over to the hospital exit, looking down the hill road. For three days he stays by the window, looking out farther inland but Emil doesn't come again.

Mikel feels himself growing stronger. He practices walking and climbing the steps at the far end of the hospital with a crutch. He climbs to the top and down and to the top again. He has never been up here before. It is a wide hallway with oil paintings on the walls. There is one of a traveler leaving his home. Another of a distant pale tree. He stops at a still life. His mouth waters at a peach. A pear.

Karine shows him where she has been staying. She takes him farther down the hallway and opens the door. It is a tiny room that was once used for storage. It has a narrow window and on the floor there is a sea of blankets. He cannot explain why but he doubts that anyone else knows she is sleeping here.

You can stay here for a while, she says, unbuttoning the top of her shirt and heading in.

They will only do this a few times.

They sit on the floor, leaning against a wall. She shuts the door with her foot. She takes out a syringe and offers some to him and then gives herself the rest. She takes his arm, wraps it over her shoulder as she lies down on his lap.

Does this hurt?

He feels nothing. He is looking up at the square of light on the wall. He wants to bury his face in her hair but he can no longer move. Pinned against the wall is one of the maps they have stolen. He hasn't seen it before. There is a red circle in an area near the border to Spain. She has drawn it there, near the Pyrenees and the Basque country. It shocks him. He is suddenly cold, his body hollow.

Remember, she says. That is my mother's home.

Your home?

Remember.

He concentrates on the red circle and the valley. He thinks of a tree and that wind chime and a farm they once worked for and his parents asleep.

Karine, he says, touching her head. Can you play cards?
Cards?

His tongue is heavy. His body gone. Her eyes still as glass.

He had been just outside the blast radius that day. Of the
second mine. It wasn't the shrapnel that entered the right
side of him, taking his hand and shattering his leg and his pelvis. It was Artur's body. The doctors were unable to collect
all of the fragments. They didn't tell him this at first. Later,
they thought he would want to know. That there was the
right to know. And to explain the nerve damage and the pain
that would for the rest of his life, now and then, flare in his
hips. Mikel would never be able to bend his knee all the way.
Because Artur was in there. They asked if he understood.

This was the first month. He wasn't walking yet. In the
bed he remained motionless, thinking that he had become a
coffin. Then he grabbed a scalpel from the tin tray and began
slicing the sutures along the side of his body, reopening the
healing skin and screaming while the attendants tried to se-
date him. Through the months of morphine he forgot Artur's
name and for a time even his own.

•

Mikel is discharged at the end of February. The ICRC gives
him the crutch he has been using and some spare clothes they

have managed to find. There isn't a coat but they say it will be spring soon as though they are in charge of the weather. They say a bus will come and take him downtown if he wishes. And that they are sorry that they need the bed.

That is all they say. The staff who treated him. Most of them are French but some of them are Canadian and British and they have been here since the end of the war. They look as emptied out as he feels and they speak little French, and Mikel doesn't know English, so they all stand and smile and wish each other luck in different languages.

He has nothing else. He leans against the crutch and walks out of the hospital down through the courtyard and the garden where there is still snow. He looks for Karine but she isn't around. He looks for the old woman who slid down the lawn behind the building, but she isn't around either. Did he imagine her? There are only reflections in the windows. He almost slips on ice but regains his balance and keeps moving down toward the gate.

The street is empty. He is standing against the wall by the street, shivering. In the distance, smoke rises from chimneys. New store awnings, brightly colored, have gone up. Farther, there are dots of movement on a boardwalk. He follows the winding route of a person on a bicycle, the way the person speeds and cuts the corners. He used to do that. He had forgotten. That he was once good at riding a bicycle. How is it possible to forget this? It occurs to him that he will never ride one again. And that he no longer trusts himself. He can think of a field of flowers or a great tree but he isn't sure anymore what that means to him.

He hears the engine of an automobile. He thinks it is the bus. It isn't. It is an American car, a Ford, old and rusted, and as it slows in front of him he is choked by a sudden fear. He holds his breath. He doesn't want the window to roll down. He wants to run. Gripping his crutch, he is about to turn back toward the hospital when Mikel hears his name.

Karine is in the car, clutching the wheel with a cigarette between her fingers. He didn't know she owned a car.

I don't, she says, but doesn't say anything more.

He tucks himself into the passenger seat, throws the crutch in the back, and she drives down the hill into the city. He isn't expecting the bumps and the gaps the car drives over. He senses the tide of pain, braces for it. Karine notices. She slows. When he is comfortable again he leans back and stares through the car window at the crowded sidewalks and the new stores.

So much is new in Calais. There is architecture he has never seen before, taller buildings. They drive along the water. They pass the ships in the port and the market where steam rises from the stalls of the vendors. Hot teas and soup. Then farther down: shelves of pottery, crates of wine and fish. He looks for a lady selling lipstick. He sees a child in a coat trying to sell kites. He thinks he recognizes a sanitation worker and thinks of the dogs.

He and Karine haven't spoken. She asks if there is anywhere he wants to stop or go. She tells him there is a ship heading to England today. She knows the crew. She points to a far dock as though she has already planned this.

We can go together, she says.

She doesn't look at him. She has grown shy.

We can leave, she says. We can start again.

Keep driving, he says.

She drives. He watches as she circles the city and then after an hour he tells her where to turn. They cross a bridge. They turn onto the river road. He hasn't been here in months. The lights of all the factories are on. He sees a hangar with new cars.

Karine accelerates, driving past the bench. He doesn't say anything. He turns and sees the men there, their breaths in the air as they throw stones against the frozen river. She keeps going until the land flattens and the shantytown appears. The sky is featureless, all gray. He reaches for her arm. She veers away from the road and stops.

You live there? she says.

He doesn't respond. The snow is slow to melt out here. She keeps the car running and the windows begin to fog.

Would you like me to go with you?

No, he says. I'm okay.

She leans over him and opens the glove compartment. There is a tin box with an ampoule of clear liquid and a syringe. It isn't labeled. She asks if he wants some but he shakes his head.

It isn't too late, she says. For the ship. England.

He will always think of her like this, in a car, before she fills the syringe. Before she leans back against the seat and her smile fades. The movement of her shoulder. The words *ship* and *England*.

I'll wait, she says, already a world away from him.

He is caught by a wind when he opens the car door. He climbs down the slope, his shoes and the crutch sinking in the snow. It takes him longer but he doesn't stop and soon he is approaching the first shanties. Snowmen with twigs for arms stand on the paths. The same dog runs over to him. He greets the animal, feeling happy for a moment before it bounds away. The shantytown looks the same to him but if people recognize him as he heads down the paths they don't show it. He doesn't recognize anyone. Somebody waves but it is courtesy.

He heads to Artur and Emil's place first. He feels his heart as he does. He knocks. But Emil isn't there. He moves on, farther down, anxious for the blue of the shanty that was his to appear. When it does he knows at once that there is someone in it. He can smell food being cooked. A broth. Then, through a gap, a piece of clothing. Someone's hand. He steps up and knocks. The same piece of wood is being used as a door.

An old woman answers. Yes? She is wearing a heavy wool sweater and a hat and behind her legs, peering at him, are two children. He recognizes his blankets. Mikel is about to reach for them and say that he lives here but hesitates. He smells the warm soup and looks at the three of them and does nothing.

I left a bag here, he says instead. A long time ago. I was wondering if it's still here.

The woman grins. She is missing a tooth. He doesn't know why but it makes him think of his hand. He hides his arm.

No, the woman says. It's not here, but it's over there. The bag. He kept it for you.

She points back toward Artur and Emil's shanty.

He's still here?

Yes, of course, she says. He's at the landfill. He collects paint. Even in this weather. Did you know? He's a painter. We have a painter here.

She seems delighted by this. She asks if he wants to come in and wait here.

You can have some soup, she says.

The children have been playing with marbles. They set the marbles up, flick their fingers, and he watches as one shoots across the narrow floor and hits his shoe. He notices them looking at his arm as he leaves the marble there, thanks the woman, and steps away.

He returns to the other shanty, thinks he will wait out front by the bench, but then opens the door. Inside, on a string, are a few clothes hanging in the air. A pile of blankets are folded carefully and stacked in a corner beside a pair of spare boots. On a shelf is an unopened pack of chocolate and a tin cup with a razor. He goes to the boots, realizing they aren't spare ones but Artur's. They're smaller. He begins to see more of Artur there. A smaller shirt. A smaller pair of gloves.

Mikel finds his bag hanging on the wall. It is a small canvas shoulder bag he found in a ditch years ago. He opens it, finds his comb, his toothbrush, and an inch of toothpaste, near frozen from the cold. His playing cards are there, too, wrapped in a pair of socks. It is all there.

He wonders what Emil has been doing with it. If he wanted Mikel to have it he would have returned it to him when he visited. If Emil was the one who visited.

Mikel leaves the bag hanging on the wall and returns outside. It is now late in the afternoon and the temperature is dropping. The wind has come back. He looks up wondering if it will snow again. He walks to the center of the path and tries to spot the landfill behind the field. He considers waiting. He thinks he should wait but no one appears in the distance.

He wonders where he will go.

Mikel leaves the shanties and walks back to the road. Karine is still there. The car is still there. The engine is running. He opens the driver's-side door. Her head is tilted back, her mouth is parted, and the used syringe lies between her fingers. The small cloud of her breath rises up toward the car ceiling.

He places the back of his hand against her neck. He is mindful of the cold but he wants to touch her one more time. She seems younger to him then, much younger than she is. He wonders if he will ever see her again. He imagines a future where this seems possible. This woman who has taken care of him. This one remaining thread in his life.

He thinks of turning the engine off but he doesn't want her to freeze. It is difficult to see the distant ridges. Even the river. He hears a train. A far riverboat.

All day he has been carrying Karine's map folded in his back pocket. Looking for her before he left, he had gone up to her room and saw it there. He takes it out now and is about to place it in the car but changes his mind and tucks it back into his pocket.

Mikel returns to the road. As he leaves, the wind comes down, changing the shapes of the snowdrifts again.

Karine, 1948

She wakes to an impossible distance.

From that tunnel she has slipped into for a year, Karine struggles to find where she is. She searches for something to hold in that far perspective. She clings to a muted, steady wind. Then becomes aware that it is not wind. She breaks her gaze away. It seems to take an hour to look down, to reach for the ignition. She tries and gives up. She drops, sinks, feels a bright warmth, and stays a little longer.

When she opens her eyes again a man is looking down at her through the window. He has lifted a gloved hand toward the glass. A tin canister of some kind is under his arm. Karine smiles. He opens the door, asks if she is all right, and she reaches for him. She can't remember the last time someone asked her that.

He turns the car engine off. He came because the car fumes were visible from the field. As he leans over she can smell paint on him, and the ice in his beard claws her cheek, jolting her awake for a moment.

He is the tallest man she has ever seen. Still holding the canister, he lifts her with his free arm and without any effort flings her over his shoulder. He carries her like a sack as he walks down the slope into the shantytown. She senses the sway of her body as though it is not her own. It tickles her, and she laughs. She hears him release the canister and sees it hit the snow like a bomb, and she keeps her eyes on it for as long as she can as he walks down a lane.

The world is upside down. Shanties. Doors. If the man speaks to anyone she cannot hear. It is only the wind now. And then, surprising her, a wind chime. She wants to follow the noise but he turns, lowering her, and she is through a door into a room.

She watches as he buries her in blankets. She wonders

why, she isn't cold. I'm not cold, she says, unaware that she doesn't say this out loud and that she is trembling. She is comfortable and settles into the fabrics as the man lights a small, contained fire in the middle of the room and smoke begins to rise toward a gap in the tin roof where there is a circle of evening.

Her first days without the morphine he keeps her in the shanty, buried in blankets as she vacillates between shaking from the cold and sweating so much she believes in her delirium that a new season has arrived. She wants to rip her clothes away but the man holds her, wiping away her sweat. She sweats and yet her teeth clatter. She ruins her clothes, feels the wetness in her pants and all over.

Then the burning begins. The flames in the shanty fire have somehow leapt into her. She screams as it cooks her from the inside and then it turns into ice that she is convinced she must break to get her blood to work again. She hits her arms. She rakes her fingernails over them. She doesn't stop until all the ice has broken.

Five days this goes on. She bleeds all over a blanket from her scratching and the man tries to protect her wrists with torn pieces of a shirt. He heats soup if he has it or boils rice or even soaks stale bread in hot water, forming dumplings the size of pebbles for her to swallow. She is always vomiting. She tries to flee, crawling half out of the shanty, and begs a frightened woman for morphine. He cleans the floor. He wraps more pieces of torn clothes around her limbs. He never leaves.

He is at times Mikel. Other times he is her brother. Other times Karine believes she is at the hospital and this man is a doctor. In the last days, when the nausea and the vomiting begin to recede, when she begins to surface, she feels grateful for him and keeps calling him The Doctor.

She no longer shakes. She feels her blood again. She is aware that she has slept. She tastes. Touches. She is dressed in clothes that aren't hers. A man's clothes. She is in a room with a hole in the ceiling where the weather and light funnel down.

Karine gets up. She wraps a blanket around her shoulders and steps outside for the first time in six days, walks up and down the lanes of the shantytown, surrounded by her own breath in the cold. Alone, she watches a man appear from the distant landfill, pushing a cart.

You don't have to go, the man says, and she wonders if it is the first time he has spoken to her—she tries to remember, searching for any recognition of his voice, which is calm, shy.

That night she leaves the shanty again. He doesn't follow her. She can see him watching through the open entrance. She crosses into the sloped field toward the main road. There is a low moon beyond. The car is no longer there, the tracks covered in fresh snow. Wrapping the blanket tighter over her, she looks toward the city and then in the opposite direction, deeper into the country.

Karine doesn't go. Not right away. Winter passes for her in the shantytown with him. She learns his name. She walks with him every day to the landfill and they collect whatever they can. Food. Paint. Insulation. She accompanies him through the shanties and as he stands to the side she asks if someone needs anything done.

Emil will do whatever they ask. Fix a roof. Build a new door. She helps him plug in holes in walls with pieces of wood or sometimes pieces of a tire. They chop wood or pile sheets of galvanized metal to sell or barter with. They collect snow in buckets and melt it.

They are paid with food, utensils, and trinkets. Someone gives her a music sheet and she holds it for a while, stilled by a note of memory.

They learn nothing about each other, the way she has learned nothing about so many people she has encountered over the years. She isn't even sure if half the time the Romanian understands what she is saying. But in the shantytown they are always together, sharing everything they find or earn, and every evening he turns so they sleep feet to head around the small fire.

Some days Emil is weak the way she was weak, when it feels as though he has lost himself in a private fortress, and as her energy returns to her, she takes care of him instead. She cooks for him. She wraps him in blankets. She kisses him. She tastes the chalk of his tongue and runs her hands across his stomach. Sometimes she does it quickly and other times she teases him a little, drawing the pleasure out for him, and listens to the gentle whimper of his voice and feels his own hands on her as shadows pass over them.

In the nights when she cannot sleep she thinks of Mikel. Not of the time she spent with him as much as the first time she saw him, the way he had walked in. The truck had left him at the gate and sped away. The only survivor. His body splattered with that intimate color. How he kept asking for a handkerchief.

There's something on my face, he said to her as she ran to him.

His mind unaware that he was walking with a shattered

leg and a broken pelvis. That his hand was gone and that he was reaching for her with nothing.

She doesn't tell him that there are days in the landfill when she searches for needles. Ampoules. If Karine ever finds one she would probably break it with her teeth and drink it. She begins to distract herself by talking about other things, finding that old desire for other lives she lived before this one.

She tells Emil that her father took care of horses near the Belgian border. That her mother was born at the opposite end of the country, near Spain, on a farm that once cultivated flowers. Poppies and lavender. That her brother used to wake her in the morning by sneaking outside and leaning through her open window like some ghost.

She says all this and wants him to understand the intimacy of memory, a person's history. She wants him to care, knowing secretly that it is for herself that she shares all this. To convince herself that she has a history, that one exists.

He never says anything back. It is as though he hasn't heard. He takes her hands and together they walk over the hills of debris and the garbage as though they are the last people on this earth and he cannot be more content.

One day she asks this man whom she has lived with for

over a month what he was before all this. Where he is from. If he knew Mikel. She asks him whose clothes she is wearing, knowing they are too small to be his own.

He grows angry. He shakes his fists and tightens his mouth and she doesn't know why until he says, Before all this? He mocks the way she said this. As though *the before* was better, he says, his voice different now, louder than she is used to.

When he hits her, once, he is as surprised as she is. She sees it on his face. The way it falls in shame. She approaches him, ignoring the circle of heat pulsing on the side of her face. She isn't angry. She tells him she isn't. She takes his hands, not expecting him to hit her again, but he does, striking her in the same spot and as she bends over, stunned, he grabs her shoulders and pushes her down the landfill. She tumbles, spins, feels a cold bright snap against her head. Blinded by a dizziness, she thinks she is vomiting. Before she can focus and rise he is on her and has pinned her down. She hears the crush of a metal can as he lies on top of her and struggles with her clothes. Cold air hits her torso.

You don't have to go, he says, the way he said it the first time, and he keeps saying it as she twirls her fingers around something beside her hip that has the texture of hair.

There is a wetness dripping down the side of her face and she has to shut one of her eyes. She lets go. Fumbles.

Tries again. She finds something to grip. The weight of him presses into her. Karine screams. She swings. Feels the ping of impact, the shock of it traveling up her wrist. She thinks he will shout or cry in pain the way the convalescents did at the hospital but he doesn't. He rolls to his side and looks up at the sky as though unsure of what has just happened.

When she stands she almost trips on her pants that are twisted around her ankles. She falls on her knees over him and swings down, overwhelmed by a fury she is unaware existed within her. Or was unaware could escape her. She swings with whatever it is she is holding and she swings down again, listening to him shouting now and screaming until she realizes he isn't saying anything at all but that it is her own voice. It was always her own voice.

She stops. She looks down. His ruined face. A bubble of air forms around his ripped lips. She cannot see his eyes. There is pulp in one of his sockets. He no longer has a nose. She stumbles back.

Emil moves. He is still alive. He tries to stand but he can't, so he crawls away from her, limb by limb, sinking farther into the camouflage of the landfill.

It is the last time she ever sees him. Karine waits for him in the shanty for a day. She takes the bag hanging on a nail on the wall. In the bag is a deck of cards, a comb, and a near-empty tube of toothpaste. She packs clothes, a pocket mirror, and the sheet of music. She heads out toward the main road. Her boots sink in the field where there are still islands of snow.

She walks, away from the city, as cars pass. Trucks pass. No one stops. She keeps walking, farther into the countryside as the light begins to dim. She walks to warm herself. She thinks of heat.

At the end of the day, Karine hears a train.

Her body is stiff and sore but she runs toward the tracks as the train rushes by her and she sees the women and the men in the last freight car that is missing a door, and she grips the hand that is reaching down for her and is pulled up.

The train continues south. She stays awake with the moon, the long, broken fields. Damage from old fires. Through the evening more passengers disembark and others get on. From the edge of the car she follows the distant approach of two children, hurrying. She helps them up. All these people still returning, even now, to what remains of their homes or going somewhere else, to start again, settle somewhere new.

The train rattles and shakes. The woman behind Karine

has been holding her so that she doesn't fall. This stranger who reached for her as soon as the train began to turn.

She will never know what this woman looks like. Whether she is old or young or her own age. To her the person will forever be only the shape and the pressure of an embrace. Red dirt under a thumbnail. A woven bracelet that carries a strand of hair.

All night they travel like this. Then Karine unlocks the arms of the woman, jumps, and enters the first moment of the morning.

•

Karine avoids Paris and stays to the northern coast. And then in the following days she begins to head south, down the western side of the country toward Bordeaux. She hops more train cars. She catches lifts on the back of pickup trucks with aid workers or migrants heading to a vineyard or other farms to earn some money.

Horses gallop after a truck she is on. It is as though she has never seen a horse before. She is stunned by them. For two beats she is convinced her father will appear. There are mounds of fresh dirt in the paddock. Covered holes from mortar rounds and other artillery fire. She watches as the horses still avoid those spots, leaping over them or going around as they chase after the truck until they are blocked by a fence.

April, far from the harvesting season, but a vineyard needs help racking. So for a few days Karine works in the labyrinthine cellars, siphoning wine from one barrel to another, leaving the sediment behind.

She is surprised a vineyard has survived. It is managed by an elderly couple and on occasion, as she works, she can see them from the high, narrow windows in the cellar. She stops working and follows them, from window to window, past the other workers who ignore her. She catches the sight of the couple's boots and the matching gait of their walk and as they move toward a hill she sees them whole, their carefulness and yet their energy as the man picks weeds from the grass and the woman claps, startling some birds she doesn't want disturbing the garden.

They pay little but they offer meals and shelter. She eats cheese and bread and olives and wine. The flavors and the richness of it all almost makes her cry. She tries to control herself, eating slowly, and avoids the eyes of everyone else as they gather in the barn, by the cots, where they will sleep. Metal drums stand scattered around the floor, filled with wood they can burn if they are cold in the night.

She lies on a cot beside a woman who talks in her dreams.

Still hungry, Karine sucks on her fingertips, tasting the salt of the olives and the tannins of the fermenting wine. She thinks if a vineyard has survived then somewhere in this country there is still a field of poppies and lavender.

Wood cracks and falls apart in the drums. Someone coughs into a bale of hay.

When I am scared, I think of that, the dreamer beside her says.

•

She keeps going. She heads south, riding in the back of more cars and walking. At an inn, she walks in, checks the calendar on the wall, steals a pencil, and starts to record the dates on the back of the music sheet.

On a warm night in May, Karine finds a tree to rest under and falls asleep, listening to the wind, covered in the sway of shadows.

She wakes to the sound of an engine. Then the engine turning off. Still lying under the tree, Karine watches as a man unzips his trousers by the road and urinates. He is smoking a cigarette and he squints from the smoke and the sun.

Hearing the stream of urine, she is suddenly freezing. She shivers. She can't feel her body. In her drowsiness she tries to remember the night before in case it is some reaction to morphine. But no, she hasn't touched it. She is just cold, sleeping outdoors, and as she gets up the man sees her and shouts.

Mierda, he says, quickly zipping up his pants and spitting out his cigarette.

Karine, warming herself under the sun, approaches him. The Spaniard is blushing and refuses to look at her. He is wearing a Basque beret, and she wonders if he was in the Resistance, a maquisard, like Mikel. She recalls slipping a beret on him once at the hospital, thinking he would want it but he didn't, he threw it back into the room where they saved the clothes of the dead to use.

The car the Spaniard is leaning on has the cloth flag of the ICRC cross on the door. There is a Red Cross armband on him, too. For a moment she believes she is wearing hers but then remembers.

She hasn't yet noticed the two others in the car. A man and a woman. The window rolls down. The other man could be Spanish, too, but begins to speak in English. So he is an American. He is asking if she is all right, though she isn't quite certain. He mimics shivering and wraps his arms around himself. The woman beside him laughs. Karine hasn't spoken English in a long time. Her mind reaches for some words.

Can I come with you? she says.

Not sure you want to go that far, the American says.

He looks like a Spaniard to her. There is something about him she cannot place, pin down. The woman who laughed has yet to speak but she is wearing an armband, too. She leans across the man and says, We're on our way to the border. You can come with us as far as you need to.

She says all this in French. Karine reaches for the front car door but the Spaniard stops her.

Your bag, he says.

I'm sorry, the French woman says.

Karine opens her bag for the man to inspect. He shakes the C rations she bought a week ago and asks her about the playing cards and the music sheet. She doesn't answer. He taps her arms. She can sense him regaining his pride as he grins like a boy and slowly runs his hands over her. She doesn't move. He lets her in, and they go.

The American's name is Oliver. The French woman is named Camille. They say they are aid workers but they have no supplies. She thinks the truck is too small to carry much but perhaps they are a part of a larger group. They say they are heading into the Basque country and Spain. Koldo, the driver, is their guide.

Karine's wrist itches. Perhaps something bit her while

she slept. But the car is pleasant and she leans back in the seat and looks up at the light in the cypresses.

Koldo asks where she wants to go.

She says, Le Sen.

They are between Bordeaux and Bergerac and by her guess they are only two hours away.

She has yet to decide whether she trusts everyone in the car or no one.

Koldo knows the town. He says, Okay.

It takes four. It takes all day. They roll down the window and smoke cigarettes. It is an old Peugeot, low to the road, and she feels every bump and the shake of the axles as they navigate craters and fallen trees and sometimes the road not even there, indistinguishable from the field. The bridge they believe existed over the Garonne was blown and no one has yet to rebuild it. They drive over wood planks that cover a narrow, dirt lane, and one of the planks caves, swallowing the corner of the car. Oliver, Camille, and Karine get out and attempt to push the car out.

As she helps, Karine looks down and catches, in the hole below, the remains of a horse, an eye looking back. Oliver sees it, too. They keep pushing until the car finds traction again and speeds down the lane for a short while. Koldo waves his cigarette in the air and honks. She looks at the horse one more time. Two airplanes fly by, their long shadows moving over the hills.

In Le Sen, they find an inn. They are the only ones there. It is on the corner of the short, cobblestone street that is the center of the town, and she wonders if her mother walked these streets as a child, whether the inn was there, what on this street was here when she was. She knows only the town's name from her memory. It was her mother's nearest town.

She is restless. The aid workers are starving and eat at the café connected to the inn. No one else is there. The innkeeper arrives and tends the bar. There is dried meat on the menu and they order all of it, plus three carafes of wine, and they eat while Koldo makes jokes about the day and the drive.

They are all tired and Karine stands, approaches the café windows. The sky is clear, nearing dark. The streets are empty except for a boy who is kicking a ball around. Some lights are on and she hears the faint murmur of a radio. There is little evidence of a war here. Or little she can see. One of the lucky towns, she thinks, and then wonders what that even means.

Across the room, Koldo has found a portable record player at the bar and pesters the innkeeper to play some records the Germans have left behind. It is American music. Ella Fitzgerald. It reminds her of the hospital. An American nurse who used to scat to an imagined song after every surgery, shutting her eyes, shaking her hands, and pretending to stand in front of a microphone in the corner of the room, someone's blood still on her arms.

Koldo approaches Camille, a cigarette stuck to his lips. There is always a cigarette stuck to his lips. She will remember this. He shakes his hips. Camille reaches for his beret and puts it on her and they dance, a little drunk, maybe a lot, and the bartender smiles and Oliver drinks his wine, watching. She watches Oliver and believes that a year ago she would have approached him at this moment, sat down, or danced with him.

She should stop drinking wine. She feels the sudden desire to be in the slipstream of morphine. Surprised at how fast it always hits her. She takes out another cigarette from Koldo's pack. The boy from outside is now peering in, his hands raised to the windowpane, the ball tucked under his arm. She waves but he backs away and runs down the street, away from the town.

Was her mother ever in this café, smoking? Did she ever sit beside someone at a table? Did she ever smoke? She never spoke of her life here. Only the flowers. Or perhaps she did.

Karine wants to build a narrative. Or remember a lost one. But she can't imagine her mother as a girl, not yet.

She approaches the bartender and shares a name, asks if he knew the family. He shakes his head and wipes the bar. As she crosses the room again, around Koldo and Camille who are still dancing, she pictures a young woman moving east across a country for a man and for children. Mama, the future nurse at a Belgian hospital. Papa the horse breeder who was traveling through here, selling horses. She sees her brother again reaching for her through the open window, waking her with the smell of the lake on his arms. The abandoned church they used to explore together, climbing the stones, though she can't remember now where that was.

And who are these people she has come here with? She sits beside Oliver, this man casually drinking his wine, and recognizes that her life these past four years has been moments with strangers. Or perhaps it always was. What terrifies her is that she doesn't know if this makes up a life. She says this to Oliver, surprised by her own openness. She is unsure if she says it the way she wants to in English, whether it sounds like something else but it seems to her like the only honest thing she has said in years.

Oliver stubs out his cigarette. He tells her he saw Ella once on a ferryboat on the Hudson River. She didn't want to be recognized, so she was wearing a long-brimmed felt hat that fluttered in the wind. He says: The bird comes, swoops down, thinks the hat's food, snatches it with its claws, and away it goes, this blue hat, Ella's hat, high above the river, into the valley.

He finishes his wine and pours more. She likes that he is calling the great singer by only her first name. She likes the intimacy of it.

I swear, he says. Even the sound of surprise in her voice sounded like song.

So he is from New York. There is this, something she knows about him. A river. A ferryboat. The small scar across his nose, the origin of which could be as plain as a branch or as romantic as a novel.

Karine asks if he wants to dance. Oliver laughs.

Not at all, he says.

If he was at all curious about her he no longer shows it. He drinks more wine and smokes. The innkeeper flips over the record. As the music plays again, Oliver is gone somewhere in a far room in his mind.

She leans into his shoulder, smelling the sourness of his shirt collar. Only this. She watches the other two, who are like trees in a lazy wind. She feels everyone's exhaustion along with her own and she wonders for how long these three strangers have been in France. Her wrist itches again. She wonders what it is.

She asks about the scar. Ella Fitzgerald sings.

She shares a room with Camille. Camille pays for it. They are on the top floor and have each taken a narrow bed. Their feet face the window. Camille, drunk, shares some dirty French jokes, pleased to be speaking in her native language. She doesn't wait for Karine to laugh. She laughs on her own and the room fills with her sleepiness.

Karine turns to her side and asks if they are really aid workers. Camille laughs again. She doesn't say anything for a while. She kicks away the covers and stares up at the night-time ceiling.

She says, more quietly now, We're looking for the American's brother.

Brother?

Well, I guess he was already found. We're going to identify the remains. Well, no. I already identified them. I'm taking Oliver so he can bring his brother home. Though it won't happen the way he imagines. The body. It's in bad shape. I'm sorry. I laugh when I'm drunk.

She covers her mouth and lies still again, her body pale as snow. In the silence, Karine drifts, holding on to some fragment, some memory, the old noises of the inn. She is back at the hospital searching. She is in a wheelchair. She finds Oliver's brother half buried in trash, his eyes gone.

She wakes from this, splashes water on her face, and leaves early. She follows the street away from the town. A house light is on. She wonders if it is the boy but it is a man asleep on a rocking chair, his spectacles hooked over a finger and dangling close to the floor.

She keeps walking. The street curves up a slope and she enters a valley. In the high distance, near the ridge, she catches the smoke from a fire. She thinks she can make out a rooftop there but she is unsure. She follows the road, farther into the valley, reaching a long field where there is a stone cottage. It appears to be the only structure breaking the distance. She spots a well. A tree out front. If there had been flowers they are gone but the house appears to have survived.

Karine sits down at the edge of the field, facing the distant property, waiting for movement. She has no idea if this is the place. The morning comes and spreads over the grass. She plucks a blade and chews on it. When nothing happens Karine makes her way across. It is colder here than in the town, windier. As she passes the tree she reaches up to touch a branch.

There is a bench with a bucket near the front door. The door cracked open. A few windows broken. She stays outside at first, circling the perimeter. She goes around the main house and gazes out at the field beyond where there is a wrecked airplane, one of its wings in the air and the other snapped into pieces in the grass. The painted flag on the tail is visible though she doesn't know what country it belongs to. When she heads down she is careful not to touch it as though the metal is still hot.

And then she does, stepping up onto the wing and peering down into the cockpit. The control panel and even the seat have been stripped and taken, scavenged for the black market. She can smell the faint trace of something burned. She gets back down and leans on the wing. She looks around, at the flat landscape, then up at the far mountain where there is smoke again.

She stays on the wing for a while and then heads back up, entering the cottage, to the dusty furniture, the long kitchen table, teacups. Pillows. An oil painting hangs tilted on the wall. There are also leaves piled up everywhere. An eggshell from a hatched bird. The smell of past seasons. Each corner like some abandoned story.

She wanders the corridors. She checks the rooms. In the first she finds long scratch marks. She bends down, spreads her hands, matches her fingers with the lines. Beside these lie a set of wind chimes. She picks it up and holds it to the light. It is as though a storm had picked it up from the tree outside, or from her mind, and carried it in.

She approaches the last room. She slides open the door. She stops. Holds her breath as she stumbles back. Her hands tremble. She grips them and breathes through her mouth. She looks in again.

In the far corner there is a figure on his knees. His head is bowed. The sun is falling on the old jumpsuit he is wearing, his hair nearly gone, the discolored, shriveled skin of his neck. She covers her nose with the sleeve of her shirt and goes closer. She turns to face him. As she does she feels a touch on her shoulder and screams.

Mierda, Koldo says, pinching his nose, looking down at the corpse.

He wraps his arms around her. He covers her eyes. She lets him, leaning into him as he brings her out. He brings her out to the bench where she vomits into the bucket. Bile and wine slosh in the tin. Koldo holds back her hair.

Come on, he says, in French. Let's go.

Karine shakes her head. She spits. No.

We're leaving soon, he says. You can come.

No, she says.

He stands in front of her. He is looking at the years of grief contained in her face and her body.

Come with us, he says, and his voice grows softer.

When she doesn't answer Koldo lights a cigarette, gives it to her, and lights one for himself. He stands there thinking. He checks his watch. He examines the door of the cottage, tries to shut it. He looks through the broken windows.

You have your bag? Your rations?

Yes.

He takes off his beret and puts it on her head.

Then I'll come back. After. Keep your head warm.

He walks toward the tree where he has parked his car. The engine is still running. He circles the tree, accelerates out toward the main road, and is gone.

Karine returns to the last room. She sits beside the pilot. She doesn't know what to do. She stays in the room as though it will tell her. He managed to take his helmet off. It is there, beside him, like the replica of a planet.

She is afraid to touch him. But she does, holding his remaining hand, the brittle dark skin, wondering what happened. She lifts the body, shocked by its lightness. She pulls it out of the room, down the corridor, and out of the house. She takes a shovel from the shed and digs. She digs behind the cottage, facing the airplane. She digs as deep as she can, until she can no longer feel her arms, and she buries him. She stumbles back inside the cottage and sleeps.

She sleeps a full day. She sleeps on the bench by the kitchen table, forgetting that there are beds in the rooms. When she wakes it is late afternoon. She wakes scratching her wrist. She looks out the window and wonders if she imagined the smoke rising from the valley ridge.

From the bag she pulls out the music sheet. She unfolds it on the kitchen table, beside the pocket mirror. The playing cards she places on a shelf.

Then she cleans the house. Or as best as she can. She finds a broom and sweeps. She collects the leaves and the eggshell and the broken bits of wood and all the years that have accumulated in pieces and brings them outside. She hangs the wind chimes. She ignores her hunger as her body slips into the rhythm of cleaning the house, the ease of it, so she keeps working.

She will have to find a way to cover the windows. In the shed she finds seeds and a wheelbarrow. Ceramic pots. A bicycle with flat tires. Ignoring the tires, she practices riding it, luxuriating in the movement. She circles the tree. The wind chimes clatter and clang as she hits them. She goes back to clean the cottage some more and then rides the bicycle again until the day starts to end.

Even in the cold she washes her clothes in the bucket outside. She has nothing to wear, so she doesn't wear anything. She watches her breath leave her in bursts. The road. She thinks about a map she once owned and wonders if it is still at the hospital. Whether the circle she drew points to where she is now or whether she was wrong, whether she is now somewhere else. She wrings water out of the clothes that were never hers. The water cools the itching in her arm. It keeps her awake. Clear.

In the kitchen she finds a rusted bread knife. She balances the mirror on the table and begins to cut her hair. She cuts it until it is the length of her chin. She stares at the face as though it isn't a reflection but someone else by a window. She smiles.

Waiting for the clothes to dry, wrapped up in a blanket, Karine eats a C ration. The strange paste of food and biscuits and chocolate. It all tastes like nothing to her. She eats another, opening cabinets and drawers filled with utensils, plates, bowls, listening to things clatter, echo, and doing it again to hear the sounds once more.

Her second night in this new place. When she is done she goes back and forth from the well to the bathtub inside until it is half full and then boils as much as she can on the stove. She climbs in, bringing the mirror and the knife in case she needs to cut her hair some more. She lowers her head, submerges herself. A shadow passes overhead. She rises, quickly, looks around. She can hear the water dripping from her hair. Then the cooing of the bird that has slipped in from the door that won't stay closed. The bird settles on a ceiling beam near her, tilts its head, flies away again.

She thinks of the pilot. Who he was. If someone is looking for him.

Karine pours more water into the tub. She brings the mirror toward her and searches her own face for some part of her family, unwilling to admit that there are days when she cannot remember them.

The bird flies in again. The wind blows the door wide open and from the tub she has a view of the tree. The night.

She tries to recall the last time she felt this kind of silence. The last time she was this alone. She scratches her wrist. She wonders what it is. She is no longer sure what to do anymore. Where to go. How to be. She presses down on the skin. She is startled by some piece of bone or shard that is loose in there, under the skin. She picks up the bread knife and presses the tip against her wrist. She presses until her skin breaks and in the nighttime she sees the slim, new river along her arm, the way it follows her wrist and swirls into the water. The cool sting. The heat. She inserts the tip of her finger into the incision and begins to search for whatever is there. She pushes down.

But there is nothing there. Another gust of wind. She hears the hinges of the door. She looks down at her finger inside her wrist and the blood coming out and the water now all dark and she shouts and begins to cry. She keeps shouting and crying as she reaches for the towel. She wraps her wrist and holds it hard. The burn and the pulse of it dizzies her. She gags. She thinks she is going to pass out. With her teeth she ties a knot as tightly as she can, and then it is done and she lowers her arms into the water.

She breathes. She calms. Through the door a light appears high in the valley. It is where she saw smoke yesterday. It is a window, perhaps. Or still a fire. She lies in the tub, holding her wrist, and stays up with it.

The morning is bright and clear. She finds another towel, cleans the wound, and wraps her wrist again. Even though there is no one else, she does this in the corner, hidden from view. She passes the tub but avoids looking at the water that is still there. She puts on her clean clothes. She drinks what is left of the kettle water.

She wonders what she will do today. As she steps outside a man appears on the valley road. He is walking with a casual slowness and when he is closer she can spot the basket he is carrying and the rifle slung over his shoulder. He turns into the field, approaching the tree, and she lifts a hand for shade and sees it is not a man but the boy she saw out the window at the inn. She makes her way toward him, and they meet under the tree.

The boy lifts the basket toward her, grinning like a sailor who is visiting a port.

Is there morphine? Karine says.

What?

Morphine.

No. Are you hurt?

No.

He eyes her wrist.

What happened there? he says.

Kitchen accident, she says. What happened there?

He blushes. He hides his hand that is missing a thumb.

I can still shoot, the boy says.

They haven't moved from the tree. He has pale hair and is wearing rubber boots and a hunting jacket too large for him. He hits the wind chimes and they listen.

Are you maquis?

What?

He points to the beret she is wearing.

No, she says, and takes it off.

Karine introduces herself. They shake hands.

His name is Luc. He is eleven. He lives up there, he says, and points to where she saw the window and the fire.

Are you alone? she asks.

He shrugs. Sometimes, he says, but doesn't elaborate. You live here? Now?

She thinks about how to respond to this. She says, Yes.

So you found him? the boy says, and gestures toward the corner window of the cottage.

Yes, she says. I found him.

We saw the plane, the boy says. We saw it spin and go down. And then we saw him. He went in there. He never came out.

Luc doesn't say who he saw it with. He has grown silent. She looks across at the far field and imagines the trajectory of the pilot, his exit and his crawl as he holds his chest, which is crushed, and makes his way toward the house, unaware that he is already dead.

Luc sits down. He lifts the cloth that has been covering the basket. The boy has carried a dozen eggs, bread, cheese, and a jar of preserves. A bottle of wine. She lowers herself, careful of the pain in her arm.

You sit down like an old man, the boy says, and she laughs.

It hurts to laugh. He tears off the heel of the bread and throws it to her.

She settles under the tree with him and together they eat. She can hear him chewing. The heaviness of the rifle as he lowers it beside him.

Were there ever flowers in those fields? Karine asks.

I think so, the boy says, chewing with his mouth open. I don't know. I'm sorry. There are things I can't remember.

He taps his head and frowns. She tells him it is okay.

You must be tired, she says. From the walk.

I'm tired, Luc says.

He stops eating and lies down in the grass. He is still shy about his missing thumb and makes a fist to hide the wound. He shuts his eyes.

You can stay here if you want, Karine says.

Okay, he says.

I mean, you don't have to go back up there. If you don't want to.

I can stay?

You can stay.

And what will I do?

Do you know how to play cards? she says.

He has not opened his eyes. The shadow of the wind chimes are moving over him.

No, Luc says. I don't think so. No.

Then we'll play cards.

And then?

We'll rest. We'll sleep and we'll eat. We'll stop and we'll wait. We'll get better. We'll start again.

We'll get better? he says.

Yes.

And we'll wait?

We'll wait.

For someone?

Yes.

Someone will come?

Someone will come, Karine says, and leans back against the tree.

She watches the boy's chest rise and fall. She hears him breathing. She hears the bending branches and then the sound of a small, bright thing overhead, crossing.

GALICIA

Antje came to Spain three years ago. She worked as a hotel maid in San Sebastián, where she met Mathis and married him. He was a manager at the hotel. He was eight years older. She was twenty-four and had left Germany after her mother died. Her mother had been in Kabul, serving as an engineer in the Bundeswehr. Antje had never traveled abroad before.

Mathis lived in a bungalow in the hills. It was a single room with a small backyard and a partial view of the coast. Every morning he went for a run and then they went to work together at the hotel. It was on La Concha Bay and ten stories tall. Each room had a balcony, a large flat-screen television, and seashells in a glass bowl by the bed.

Sometimes she passed Mathis along a corridor. They kept their relationship to themselves even though everyone knew. Once, she heard two maids mention how dull he was. How plain. She admitted to herself that they weren't entirely wrong but it was what she wanted.

Mathis was kind and responsible. Considerate. He was from Paris, where his family was, and he was handsome, with his pale eyes and his trim beard. They were often together. They swam, cooked, shopped at the markets. He took her to restaurants and bought her nice lavender soap tied with a ribbon. He showed her how to garden. They left food and water out for the stray dog that sometimes visited the back-yard.

He hated to read. So she lay beside him in the evenings and read to him, practicing her Spanish, and without telling him she veered away from the story and invented her own. Some nights he noticed, pinching her. Other nights he didn't.

It never bothered her that he was older. She was still in awe of how different her life was now, how far away she was from her solitude and her boredom, a town she never felt was hers but her mother's, and now her mother's ghost.

Mathis told her she didn't have to work any longer if she

didn't want to, that he would care for her. But she liked the work, it kept her busy, and she liked heading down to the hotel with him every morning, riding on the back of his mo-torbike.

For a while they were happy. He wanted to start a family. So they did. They had a child, a boy, but they lost him after only a week. The doctor said there was something wrong with his heart. Or that was what she remembered him saying as she walked out of the hospital alone, past an ambulance rushing someone in, past the courtyard and the garden.

Antje walked and walked. She walked out of the city and along the coastal roads. She was barefoot and she walked for hours. The weakness and the pain of her body grew numb. She was bleeding from somewhere but she didn't notice. She heard cars speeding by and felt a kind of emptying, like parts of her were being unfurled into the air. It was difficult to move her eyes. The road and the sky became a single point she couldn't break through.

Then, when she couldn't go on any longer, she felt a shift inside of her. A restructuring. As though there was something new inside, somewhere beneath her ribs. Or something old she never knew was there.

When she looked up it was evening. She was sitting in the train station with her hands on her chest.

Mathis was beside her, holding her shoulders.

Let's go home, he said.

He stood and she followed him, and they returned home, and she didn't think the days would pass, but they did.

She continued to work at the hotel. Mathis did, too. They rode down on his motorbike every morning as they had done before. She accompanied him on his errands and they went to the beach for a swim. They swam parallel to the coast. Her skin darkened and her hair turned paler than she imagined it could. She kept it in a braid; it grew longer, all the way to the small of her back.

One day Antje opened the door of a hotel room to find Mathis there. She stood still, gripping her cart, unable to move or speak. He was sitting upright on the edge of the bed, in a suit that didn't fit him properly, holding the glass bowl filled with seashells. He turned. He didn't seem surprised to see her at all.

Oh, he said. I just wanted some quiet. That's all.

She would've come to him if he had asked or made some gesture. But all he did was return the bowl to the table and sit back down, and she closed the door and cleaned another room instead.

Mathis didn't come home that night. And for the rest of

that month there were nights when she remained alone. She assumed he began sleeping in the hotel room. Antje didn't bring it up; she was relieved.

She stayed in the backyard, lying on the hammock he had bought. She drank wine, read a book to practice her Spanish. She started another to learn Basque, too. She watched satellites gliding across the sky. Nights smelled like fire. Sometimes the stray dog appeared, lay beside her, and looked out at the sea.

Antje left the television on while she cleaned the hotel rooms. In each room she picked a different station. It was like entering pockets of the world, as though she were a great traveler.

When she was a child, she had often watched *The Time Machine*. The Morlocks had terrified and enthralled her. And Yvette Mimieux was the most beautiful woman she had ever seen. For a long time she was convinced that Rod Taylor was her father. That he was on a very long journey. She rooted for him.

She was making a bed one morning in the summer when an image appeared on the screen that made her stop. It was a clip of a city building with a burned hole in its side. As if the structure had rotted away. There was smoke everywhere.

A bomb had gone off in the northwest, in Galicia. It happened at dawn and the building had mostly been empty. Still, the television showed a young woman tripping over the debris as police officers rushed to her. She was wearing a blue dress. The dress fluttered and showed off her hips. The footage was shaky but it looked as though the woman was gripping her wrist. That she was missing a hand. Antje wasn't sure because the camera was far away.

She listened to the calm voice of the reporter. She didn't understand all of what he was saying, she had never heard some of the words in Spanish before, but she tried. She kept staring at the woman who by now had a blanket over her and was being taken away.

Antje jumped when a man entered the room.

The man was her age. He was wearing a dark suit. It was his room. He smelled of cologne and chewing gum. He apologized several times and then they were both silent. He glanced at her chest and her legs. He leaned against the wall. He tried speaking to her and she pushed her cart out the door, pretending not to understand.

Antje forgot to turn the television off. She could still hear it as she walked down the hall. She didn't turn, knew the man was there, staring.

She kept picturing the woman in the dress, gripping her

wrist. Was she missing her hand? She wasn't sure anymore. There had been something dripping down the side of her arm. Or perhaps that was just the dress. She wondered if the woman had been returning from a party. A late night. It seemed that way, the kind of dress you wore to a party.

The first time she ever passed Mathis in the hall, he was talking with hotel guests. She slowed down with her cart and eavesdropped on what he was saying to them. He thought she slowed for him, not for what he was saying. Then, later, she did slow for him.

All that seemed so long ago.

She went inside to an identical room and started the vacuum. She pushed it back and forth; the noise filled the air.

He said he wouldn't be gone long. Just a few days. He was attending a conference. Mathis kissed her then, quickly, and it startled her. He didn't notice.

The stray dog appeared, licking the back door and wagging his tail. They had never let him inside but she looked at Mathis and he nodded. The dog leapt onto the couch.

His name is Rofo, Mathis said. Someone told me that.

Rofo placed his head on Antje's lap. She wondered what kind of dog he was.

He's an Akita, Mathis said. Those dogs from Japan.

She buried her fingers into Rofo's fur and played with his ears. In recent months his muzzle had begun to gray.

We've never been to Japan, she said.

No, he said, no we haven't.

He rolled his suitcase to the door. She watched from the couch, suddenly missing him before he was gone.

Mathis, she said.

They smiled at each other. He seemed to her so much older then, so much older than he was. The gray had started in his hair, too. For the first time she noticed the loose skin of his hands, the visible veins.

She said, Bring me back something. A souvenir.

She said it because he used to. The house was decorated with things he had brought back from the hotel conferences: a snow globe, a set of Brisca playing cards, lavender soap, a shell from a different coast.

I will, he said, and she petted Rofo and listened to the taxi go down the road.

She went to the hotel all that week. She took on extra shifts. She had the motorbike to herself, so she spent time on the bay. It was July, the peak season, and all the hotels were full. On the beaches and the verandas there were so many languages and accents.

She smuggled some cleaning supplies from the hotel and cleaned the bungalow. She slipped into the pace of work. When she was done she stood in the center of the house and looked around at the accumulation of their life together, the three years she had been with him.

Mathis called once. They talked to each other about their days.

She fell asleep in the hammock. She woke to something licking her fingers, shrieked, looked down at Rofo underneath her. She laughed. She thought of the child. This surprised her. She hadn't done so in a while. She concentrated on the boy but nothing came; she was met with a blankness, as if someone had carried him into a far corridor she couldn't find. She kept thinking this would change, that she would discover him again as time passed.

She wanted to do better. She kept saying this to herself. That she wanted to do better.

The day Mathis was due to return, she woke early, when it was still dark. It came to her then, like an unfinished thought from a dream. She put on a pair of jeans and a T-shirt. She left food and water out for Rofo. She was carrying a small shoulder bag she found in a hotel room years ago. She took Mathis's motorbike, crossing the bridge over the Urumea.

The morning was already hot and dry. At the station,

Antje found a bench. Announcements came through on the loudspeaker. The giant timetable above her changed. On a television there was an update on the bombing, men with rifles and helmets storming a home. She waited to see if they would replay the clip with the woman in the blue dress. People entered the station and left.

She stood when the train arrived. She watched the gate. Soon, the passengers began to appear until there was a crowd, and Antje scanned their faces. Mathis wasn't there. She waited a little while longer, for the gate to empty, but he still didn't show. She sat back down. She thought she got the information wrong. She took out her phone and called but he didn't respond.

She didn't know how much time passed. She stared at her phone in her hands and when she looked up a man was staring at her from across the station. Antje didn't recognize him at first. She thought it was Mathis, of course it was him, and she waved and made her way toward him.

But it wasn't him. It was the young man from the hotel, the one whose room she was cleaning when he came in. He was wearing the same suit. His hair was combed and he smelled of the same cologne. He said, There you are! and smiled. He looked down at his shoes and kept his hands in his pockets.

Are you going on a trip? he said.

She was about to leave until she realized she was nodding. She heard her voice. She said she was. She said, Yes.

He asked where.

She looked behind him at the television, where they were showing the bombed building.

Galicia, she said, without thinking.

The young man's eyes brightened. He said that he was, too. And that the train was boarding. They must hurry. He offered his hand. And before she understood what was happening Antje took his hand and followed him. They passed through the gate. She saw her legs and feet moving down the platform but it seemed as if she weren't moving at all. Stopping at an open car, she concentrated on the softness of the young man's hand.

I am so glad for this, he said, and helped her up.

Her mother often took her on the train. Antje couldn't recall where they were going to or coming from. Only the train. And the changing portrait framed in the window: their conjoined reflection, her mother holding her from behind, and beyond that the shifting skyline. She hadn't thought of this in a long time. She leaned against the window now and watched the country appear and vanish: the churches, the fields, the sun, and all the stone.

He had introduced himself as Félix. He worked for a popular clothing company and was on his way to a textile factory in Lugo, in Galicia. She recognized the company name because Mathis had bought her one of their shirts for her birthday last winter. A shirt with printed dots she once wore to a hotel event with him, not realizing it was a formal affair. She had retreated to a corner, angry at him for not telling her until he pulled her out for a dance, not caring if people saw, and he showed her the steps patiently, as though they were alone in the room, and in that moment she loved him.

Across from her, Félix was asleep with his mouth slightly open and his tie loosened. She was surprised by his normality. There was an ease between them she wasn't expecting: they had slipped into conversation, about the clothing company, the factory, his fear of flying. He seemed different to her now than he did in the hotel. He seemed very young. And happy. He had even offered to buy her ticket when the conductor came by but she had bought her own even though she couldn't afford it.

She hadn't known what to say when Félix asked at the start of the trip how far she was going. She thought of the clothing company and said she was visiting Lugo, too, and he said, Because of the wall? and she nodded and said, Yes, I always wanted to see the wall.

It was not to be missed, he said. He apologized again for the other day, about startling her. He wanted to know about her work and the hotel and how long she had been in Spain and everything. She answered what she felt like answering, often not with the truth, and avoided what she felt like avoiding. He didn't push. The way he sat there reminded her of how some animals made their presence known, once, and then went to their corner.

She was wondering about the bombing and, as if he were reading her thoughts, he told her it was okay, it was on everyone's minds, it had happened in Pontevedra, all the way on the coast, far away. No one was killed. Only a few injured. He heard those responsible were separatists. That it was about Galician nationalism. He brought up the Basque country, where San Sebastián was. He thought the notion of discovery and exploration within us was corrupt. It was a notion of conquest. We were defined by collision.

She didn't understand him completely. She kept picturing the woman in the blue dress, holding her wrist, the colored drip like a streamer or a belt trailing behind her.

He tried not to think about it too much, he said. He believed that if we worked hard we would find our ways. He blushed at his own earnestness. He liked history, he confessed. He smiled again. She liked that he smiled often.

I am glad you're here, Félix said, and he shut his eyes and fell asleep as though he had turned off a switch.

It was a long journey but she didn't mind. She watched the morning turn into the afternoon, the daylight shift and move. Every now and then the train slowed and made stops, picking up and dropping off passengers. There were stretches when they traveled undisturbed across the country, the world moving as though a great hand were pulling her along. In the last few years it had always seemed like she was the one moving. She settled into her seat, facing the stranger across from her, and her eyes grew heavy and closed.

Her body shook. She woke, thinking she was falling, and grabbed the armrests. At first she didn't recognize the train car she was in or even where she was. The sun was still high, brightening the passing landscape and the empty seat in front of her. Then she remembered Félix. Saw him clearly in her mind. Where had he gone?

Gripping the seat, Antje looked around at all the passengers in the car. She wanted to speak but no sound came. She was unaware that she was holding her breath until the train shook again and she surfaced.

Félix appeared, walking slowly down the aisle with two cardboard trays. They were filled with beers and sandwiches.

He said he hoped he hadn't startled her. He was wondering if she was hungry. She was. She hadn't eaten all day. She took a bite of the sandwich and another, calming. She drank the beer. Félix had combed his hair and tightened his tie. She smelled toothpaste on him.

We're almost there, he said.

They had crossed into Galicia while Antje slept. They were now approaching Lugo from the north. They passed highways and a soccer field. Concrete high-rise buildings painted in different colors, a bright orange, a green. Silos. It was almost six o'clock but it still looked like morning outside, the summers much longer here. Félix tapped a finger against the window, at a large building in the distance.

The factory, he said. We're going there.

She didn't correct him. She saw the wall. It surrounded the town. She had never seen anything like it before. It was as though they were approaching a kingdom. There were high gates and towers and the remnants of enormous turrets.

Roman, Félix said. They're Roman. Third century. There used to be a moat. Imagine.

She pictured the moat and the sentries and all the villagers. The king and the queen. The days and the wars. And then the train entered the Lugo station and they were disembarking and moving quickly down the platform. Sitting in the car, she had grown used to keeping still. She took his hand again and stayed behind him as they walked through the station that resembled the one they had left—the vaulted ceilings, the timetable, the giant clock.

The factory was on the outskirts of the city, at the edge of the woods. They took a taxi. At the gate, Félix told the guard that Antje was observing, a new hire. He said all this naturally, as though he had done this before. Passing through, he winked at her.

The building was tall, modern, with many windows. On a high floor, she spotted a janitor lifting a mop. In another, a woman stepped into a glass elevator and descended. Félix knew her. They embraced at the entrance and then the woman embraced Antje, too.

Her name was Camila. She was perhaps thirty and there was a conservative beauty to her. She was wearing a dark suit and heels. Her eyes were black with mascara and she smelled of a nice perfume. She walked with quick steps as she took them on a tour.

It was after hours and the building was nearly empty. On each floor Antje could hear the faint hum of a vacuum. They entered rooms filled with worktables and machines, others with tailor's dummies and drawings. Boxes were stacked in storage, many with stamps from Indonesia and Morocco.

They weren't there for very long, less than an hour. They ended on the top floor. It was a large room that had been painted a shade of yellow. One side of it was all glass and the sun was coming through. The entire city and the surrounding woods were visible: the winding streets, the spires of the cathedral, people walking the length of the city wall.

Behind her, clothes were hanging on racks. There were dozens of them. Shirts, pants, dresses, and sweaters, all of them organized by color. Félix examined them, taking notes on a clipboard. She wondered if there was an order for how they arranged the colors. She was about to ask but then Félix told her that he had to step out for a moment. He said that he'd be back. That Camila would be here.

He said, Okay?

Okay, Antje said, and watched him go.

They were now alone, Antje by the windows and Camila by the racks. Antje followed Camila's reflection moving across the room, her heels tapping the shiny floor.

Why don't you try something?

Antje laughed. She lifted a hand and shook her head.

Camila stopped at the end of the rack. Please, she said.

She pointed to the clothes. Pick something. She was holding her smile.

The room appeared much smaller suddenly. Antje approached and browsed the clothes, moving from color to color until she reached a blue dress in a middle rack. She hesitated. It looked like the one from the television clip, sleeveless and long. The skirt swayed as she lifted it.

Perfect, Camila said, taking it from her.

She waited for Camila to show her where to change, to point to a door but she stood very still by the racks, holding the dress for her and watching.

Please, she said again, and gestured for her to go on.

The evening light had settled on the trees; it shone through the room and now on her skin as she took off her clothes. She kept glancing at Camila, whose face was expressionless. Then she carried the dress and stood in the middle of the room. The sun felt good on her naked body. She turned. It touched her neck and her chest and her stomach and it felt good. She opened her eyes. Below her, a car was leaving the factory, a guard lifting the gate. She thought the guard looked up. She thought it would bother her. She stayed by the window and stepped into the dress and she heard Camila's steps echo in the room, smelled her perfume, and felt the woman's fingers zipping her up.

Camila turned her around; she lifted Antje's hand and spun her. She took out an eyeliner pen. She said, Keep still, and drew around Antje's eyes. She told Antje to blink. She darkened and shaded. She put on lipstick and blush. She took out a pocket mirror and held it up.

Gorgeous, Camila said, and Antje smiled at her painted face in the tiny circle.

She kept the dress. She wore it that evening, stuffing her clothes into her handbag as she and Félix left the factory for the city. They had dinner in a square that had a tall water fountain, strings of lights, and live music. She wanted him to order for her. He ordered mussels and shrimp and ham and wine, and they ate with their fingers and tore off pieces of thick bread.

He didn't believe how long her hair was. She undid the braid and showed him.

She liked watching him eat. He was unaware of the crumbs on his chin, the oil on his lips. Mathis wiped his mouth after every bite. She noticed this when they first met and it hadn't changed. She found herself reaching for her phone but stopped herself. The audience clapped after a song and she clapped, too.

As it began to grow dark, Félix took her up to the wall.

They walked the city perimeter, peering down at the old buildings and the bright neon signs of the stores. She imagined again how it once was, the forests and the river, the pockets of villages and farms. She asked Félix what Galicia meant. He didn't know. He heard it was Celtic. He heard it had to do with milk. Or the hills.

She said that for someone who enjoyed history he wasn't very helpful.

He grew embarrassed and she touched his face and slipped her arm around his. She almost tripped on the path and leaned into him. They were slightly drunk. The first stars appeared. They circled the city as it transitioned into nighttime. On the wall there was a poster protesting the bombing; another, farther on, in support of it, resistencia y alegría spray-painted on the stone.

Félix was from Madrid. He was twenty-four years old, the same age as when she came to Spain. The clothing company was his family's. Next season he would travel to Morocco, to a factory there. It was a way to see the world.

Listening, it occurred to her that he and Camila were lovers. Or had been. Antje had no proof of this but felt certain all the same. She thought they made a pretty pair. She repeated the words *a pretty pair* to herself and wondered what Félix's parents were like. How much they saw each other. She had only met Mathis's parents once, at their wedding. They seemed tired to her, resigned to their child's foreign life.

She liked the feel of her arm around Félix's. The way she settled into him like a lock. This young man whom she had only known for a day.

A dog crossed their path, jumping onto the edge of the wall as though it were a racecourse. He looked like Rofo. They watched as he passed them, jumped once more, and went down the steps of the wall and out of the city toward the high-rise buildings. Lights were coming from a distance, reaching the sky and shifting.

Come on, she said.

She tried to follow the dog but lost him. She followed the strange lights in the sky. Félix caught up to her. They entered a maze of sidewalks and climbed a pedestrian bridge over a highway, heading out into the country. She forgot what time it was, whether it was early or late. She was suddenly filled with energy. She was on an unpaved road and she kept walking.

Antje, Félix said, and she ignored him.

The distant beat of music reached her. She heard her name again and she couldn't recall if she had ever told Félix her name. She thought of the day she opened the hotel room door to find Mathis sitting on the edge of the bed. The bowl of seashells. His solitude. How it made her feel like someone else. How she knew in that moment that what was broken had already existed long before they had met. How it was still with her now, here.

The music grew louder. The grass brushed against her skirt. A long breeze. Félix still behind her. She reached the ridge and stopped. A stone mansion stood in the far distance, without a roof, with broken walls. Ancient. Lights spilled from inside, across the grounds and into the air. A DJ was on a platform wearing headphones and leaning over turntables and a laptop. Hundreds of dancers surrounded him. They were all wearing bracelets and necklaces that glowed, jumping and spinning, their arms reaching into the air.

She went down and made her way through the crowd. She lost Félix. She climbed over what had been a wall to a room. She thought she saw Camila, reached for her, but it was someone else, someone much older. She watched a boy's body moving as though he were tied by strings. And in the shifting light she saw that there were other rooms and halls, the remnants of them extending across the field, all of them filled, and Antje danced and stepped farther in.

What could it have been? What had Félix offered her? She had known so clearly that morning; she had been so sure.

Later, watching him from across a hotel room, their clothes damp from sweat and their bodies still carrying the energy of that field, she kept waiting for it to return, wanting it to, like a thing she could grasp and swallow. Paint herself with. Then in the morning, as he slept, Antje changed back into her clothes, hung the dress in the closet, and left his room, shutting the door.

She never saw him again. She went to the rail station and took the first train heading east. Lugo and its city walls slipped away from view. She sat by a window and thought of Mathis, wondering if he was in a town like the one she had been in, if he was alone. She tried calling him. She counted the rings. When it prompted her to leave a message, she began to talk, telling him where she was, where she had been, unaware that she was speaking in German.

The train crossed the country. Antje slept. Dreamed. She swallowed a ball of thread and the ball exploded quietly inside of her. She felt a great relief that she had contained it. In the weeks after they had lost the child, Mathis had come to her, lying on top of her, and she had let him for a while; and then it grew unbearable and she struck him and pushed.

He didn't touch her again, not that night or the night after, and the days went on but she was never able to tell him that it wasn't the child she was thinking of but the desert where her mother had been, the desert and the man approaching her mother's Humvee, his hands in the air, all their lives strapped across his torso.

She lived long enough to drag someone out of the wreckage. Her mother without her legs. Her mother the engineer.

In that last year Antje mostly saw her through a computer. On the screen she was always under a tent in the desert as though she were on holiday. The video often froze, and it was just her mother's voice and her frozen image, caught with her eyes closed.

I can still see you, her mother always said. Keep moving.

She returned to San Sebastián in the evening. It was as if she had been gone for a long time and no time at all. She breathed in the night air outside the station. A policeman and his dog were making their rounds, the dog sniffing the parked cars and Mathis's motorbike, which was where she left it.

She was heading toward the bike when a shadow frightened her. Convinced that she was hallucinating, she went still and then trembled as a monster took shape under a streetlamp. It had black eyes, pale skin, and horns, but as it approached she saw that it was a costume, and the person came up to her and bowed.

She couldn't tell if it was a man or a woman inside, young or old. The person lit sparklers and offered her one. She held it and watched as the person left and joined a group of others that had appeared, all of them wearing different costumes and waving sparklers. She thought she heard German. And then, later, other languages.

In the distance, the city had changed. She didn't see until now. There were banners hanging above the streets. New lights. A summer festival had begun.

When the sparkler dimmed, she started the motorbike and pulled out of the station. She had yet to reach Mathis; she didn't know if he was home. At the station exit, she slowed. Traffic was moving across the bridge over the Urumea.

Antje waited for an opening.

VLADIVOSTOK STATION

On my way home today I saw someone in the field, someone I once knew. I was coming down the road from a hill and saw him from a distance. Yet I knew it was him, even from afar and after so long. It was as though he had always been there, still as a tree. Kostya, with the weight of an old grief on his shoulders.

I headed down. He made his way across the field. And then he was there, in front of me, older now, with gray in his hair, but the same to me.

Misha, he said. Hello. Can I walk with you?

I was trying to recall the last time I had seen him or heard his voice. How long it had been. He had spoken to me in Russian. I wondered what he had been doing out here. It was quickly growing dark. And cold. He seemed tired but restless. There was no one else, not in the field or on the road.

So we walked. Kostya fell into step with me. I followed the road, passing under the old linden trees that we used to ride under with a bicycle, me on the seat and Kostya pedaling. If he noticed me looking at him he didn't seem to mind. He placed his hands into his jacket pockets. It was a hunting jacket that was too large for him.

You still have that bag, Kostya said.

I lifted the bag I was carrying. It was a leather tool bag that had been my grandfather's. He had bought it from a tinker the day he was released from the camp, not knowing what it was for. He just wanted something of his own, he said.

I used it every day. I packed my lunch and a book. If it was light outside, I walked home reading, something I knew I should never do but did.

A motorbike almost hit me once. I felt the rush of air and the whisper of the motorcyclist's arm as I tumbled into the field. As the engine noise faded, I saw the dim shape of a plane fly above me and thought of Kostya. It was the last time, I realized now, I had thought of him.

Here, I said. You can carry it for me.

Kostya laughed. Still the same laugh. It was nice to hear it. He took the bag from me and we continued down the road through the fields.

The evening came. We smelled the cattle farm. We had been told the winter was coming earlier this year but there was no wind tonight and the sky was open, full of stars.

I was heading to the railway, Kostya said. When I saw you, I was heading to the mill.

We called it the mill because it was once a facility for wool, but it was now a maintenance station, for the Trans-Siberian and the local lines, and I worked there. I had worked there for years. I repaired the insides of the train cars. I ripped out the old seats and bolted in new ones. I checked the safety windows, the luggage compartments. I found the things passengers dropped into the crevices—money, house keys, the backs of earrings—and I brought them to the lost and found. Because of my leg I had to rest often, but I had been there the longest and they let me work alone and at my own pace.

Sometimes I stayed on the trains I repaired and went a few stops with the conductors. I liked trying the new chairs. I liked watching the country pass. When I was a child my mother used to take me as far as Vladivostok but I never went that far now. I didn't want my father to worry.

Our home was three hours north, at the start of the valley. I lived in my father's inn. This was in Primorski Krai. The Maritime Territory. My grandparents had moved here. Kostya's had as well. They were all Korean refugees from the Second World War. They had come from the Pacific, from Sakhalin Island, where they had been forced to work in a Japanese labor camp.

After the war, when they were released, there was nowhere to go, nothing for them to return to, so they settled here, in the Far East. They found work and started families of their own.

Kostya used to work in the nearby rice fields with his father. But when his father died, he came to help at the inn my father started. It was a busy time for us. It was beautiful country, and people visited or passed through. We helped guests with their luggage or vacuumed the lobby. We cleaned the rooms together. Sometimes Kostya would notice me rubbing my leg and he would say, Misha, go rest on the bed, and he would finish for me, all the while talking about a book he was reading, an adventure story, a hunt.

He liked books. When she could, my mother would bring one back from the city for him. Then he would vanish for hours and I would go looking for him. I would walk through the fields surrounding the town, through the high grass, until

I felt something enclose my ankle like the soft mouth of a dog. I was expecting it and yet it always startled me. I slipped down and there he was, sitting there with the book on his lap. So I stayed with him.

Kostya who always slowed for me.

For a while there had been no lights along the landscape, but now we could see the distant windows of the farms and, as we headed into the valley, the town.

He asked how the leg was, and I said, Good. It's better now.

It was how we met as children. He had made fun of the way I walked.

Suddenly, there was a noise. Kostya stopped. He could always hear the planes before I did. I caught the quick shape of it flying over in the dark. I tried to make out Kostya's expression but there was just his head tilted and his eyes under the evening. He was still carrying my bag.

A military base was nearby. They often did their practice runs in the evening. I knew this because Kostya had flown with them. I saw very little of him then. He would come back during a furlough but that was all. I wasn't supposed to know where he was but I knew, knew that everyone on the base was in Chechnya during those years. The seasons grew

slower and for extra pay I started working at the maintenance station.

When Kostya came home, he stopped flying planes.
I thought he would come work with me at the station but
he stayed at the inn, cleaning the rooms. He didn't seem to
mind that there were fewer guests, less to do. I would come
home sometimes to find him cleaning a tub, trying to remove
a stain that was many years old. Kostya, I would say. It's good
enough. And he would smile and nod, put the cleaning supplies away, and head to his room.

I wondered now whether my father was worrying about
me. I wondered where Kostya was sleeping tonight. He had
yet to mention his house. I didn't want him to see it. But we
were approaching the split in the road. If we went straight
we would go down a slope farther into the valley and enter
the town. The road on the left was more narrow and still
unpaved, with a sign that directed travelers to a small lake.

I took my bag from him. I said, Kostya, where are you
staying? Let's go to the inn.

But Kostya ignored me and turned onto the dirt road.
So I followed him. It was the one road that had remained
unchanged since we were children, except for the lamps that
now shone on the path and the surrounding grass. We used
to play soccer here. Or I would try.

The lake appeared. It was the only moment tonight when Kostya walked faster than I could. I let him. He kept slipping in and out of the light of the road lamps. I could see the reflection of the mountain in the water.

We were nearing three houses that stood behind a line of trees. Kostya had been born in the middle one. I thought he would enter the short pathway toward the front door, but he simply paused and looked across at his old house and the two others, keeping his distance.

None of their lights were on. The houses had been empty and in disrepair for a while now. The roofs were broken by the winters. Sleeping bags and empty bottles littered the front lawns. Kids used the houses for parties. From the town, I could catch their flashlights in the trees or the smoke of a bonfire. Hear their music, the bottles they broke.

Kostya walked into the field toward the lake. He found an overturned canoe with a crack in its hull. He brushed the dirt and the weeds away and sat down. I sat beside him, rubbing a knot in my leg.

I'm sorry, Kostya, I said.

I was thinking of working on the house, he said. I could fix it up.

I'll help, I said.

In the dark I thought he smiled.

Yes, he said. We'll work on it.

We had lost a ball once. It floated in the center of the lake and I was the first to swim out. It never occurred to me that my leg would cramp up, and I panicked, I went down, and for a moment I felt nothing. It was as though I had found a different place, something far greater than a lake, and it was wonderful to me. I wanted to stay. But I was pulled up. Kostya dove and pulled me up.

A radio tower was blinking on the mountain. It looked like a single tree on the far ridge. On the island, our grandfathers had felled trees. Then, later, they mined coal. They were kept there for six years, through the war, never knowing where they were exactly in the world. They even met men who were unaware that they were on an island. They had left Korea in a cargo hold and arrived dehydrated and disoriented, and for six years they worked. Our grandfathers worked while the bodies of those who didn't survive were carted away. They worked as planes flew overhead, erasing briefly the sounds of the sawing and the drilling and the coughing.

Once a month they were brought to the sea. They were given time to bathe. It was the only time the guards didn't seem to care what they did. Someone always tried to escape. One person always tried to swim. The guards let them. And our grandfathers would say nothing and hurry to clean themselves as the man vanished into a swell, rose, kept going. Sometimes they would come back a month later to find an unrecognizable body on the shore, picked at by the birds.

When I was young I didn't understand what an island was. I used to believe the camp lay just beyond the mountain range. That they were right there. I used to hold my grandfather's ruined hands and feel the curve of his spine and wonder if the misshaped bones in my body were from him.

Kostya, I said. Were you looking for me? When you were on your way to the station?

The radio tower continued to blink. We hadn't moved from the canoe.

I don't know, he said. I was just looking.

He had brought nothing with him. During the war in Chechnya I used to listen to the radio as often as I could. Whenever Kostya returned I asked him how bad it was. Not bad, he always said. And in the years following I forgot that he had gone at all, the two of us living together at the inn the way we did when we were younger.

I used to hope that he would take me into the air but he never did. I would get angry at him. I would act like a child. And he would let me. He would stand there and let me say things to him. And I remembered this now. And I remembered how much I had once missed him.

Something skimmed the surface of the water. We heard it. We followed the wake.

It was bright in the town but the streets were empty. Only the grocery store was open, with a song playing on the radio. A boy pedaled by on his bicycle, turning to look at us as he passed. We watched him vanish into an alleyway.

Where has everyone gone? Kostya said.

I looked at the houses we were passing. I had not been looking at them lately. I didn't know. Novosibirsk. Vladivostok. Farther. Seoul. Tokyo. Shanghai.

My father's inn was three stories tall and the last house on the street. The sign was lit but the inn was closed. He had begun to close it in the evenings, retiring to his room earlier. I looked up to see if he was awake but his window was dark. He had left the entrance light on for me, which he always did.

I turned the locks, and as we went inside we were met with the familiarity of a place that we had known all our lives: the fireplace and the furniture, the striped wallpaper.

Is he asleep? Kostya asked, and I nodded, putting down the bag in the hall.

He'll want to see you, I said, but Kostya raised a finger to his lip.

The air felt stale to me. I went and opened a window, reminding myself to shut it before the morning.

Kostya hung his jacket on the rack the way he always did before fetching the cleaning supplies from the closet. How diligent he had been. How hard he had worked under my father.

With a lightness he now stepped around the desk and turned the television on. The sound blared, briefly, before he muted it. A game was on. It was a game from a week ago that I had already seen.

He settled into the chair, wide-eyed, and watched. It was as though he had not seen a game in a long time. Inside, under the ceiling lights, I could see the years on him: his thinning hair, the wrinkles around his eyes. His frayed clothes. He was thinner than I remembered, gaunt.

I went into the kitchen and looked for some food. I made us cheese sandwiches with mustard. I brought the plate and two beers to the desk. He reached for the sandwich without looking and took a bite and drank the beer.

The clock read eight o'clock. It had felt earlier to me. I didn't know where the hours had gone. I wanted to talk to him but I didn't know what to say. I gathered a stack of bills I had yet to pay and put them on a shelf. Then I sat at the edge of the desk. He kept staring at the silent television.

Kostya, I said. Where have you been?

I could see his eyes track the ball across the field.

Kostya, I said again.

I gave up. I was suddenly aware of the age of this house under the old lights, the old wallpaper and the old wood and the old smell in the air. The outdated television. I was suddenly embarrassed. I didn't know why I had brought him here. I didn't know what to do. I stopped.

There was a photo on the desk. It was of my mother, Kostya, and Kostya's father. They were in front of the inn, their hair wild from the wind. My father had taken the photo. I could never remember where I was on that day.

Do you ever think of her? Kostya said.

Then he said my mother's name and it startled me. I drank my beer. I couldn't remember the last time someone had spoken it out loud, the last time I had heard it.

She was a teacher at the local school and I used to wait for her to appear down the street, wait for her to come back to the inn. Even though she was tired from her day she would take me around town, and if she had money for it she would buy me an ice cream.

But most days she brought me back to the school, to the room where there was a piano. She would unlock the blue door and sit beside me and teach me scales, her hands moving across the keys like birds. Then I watched as she played something from memory, never sure where she had learned to play or who had taught her.

She did this every day in her last year with us. How I loved approaching that door. The shape of it, like the hull of a ship. The way she would stand there in front of it and tell me to wait as she looked up and down the hall, fumbling for her keys. To sneak in and play the school's piano with me. As though preparing me and herself for some new future.

It was strange to think of them now, her and my father. To think of what promise they had contained in each other. The son of Korean refugees and the Russian woman who was staying at the inn one day. The woman who had come back.

That was all I knew of that story. They had me. They had tried.

It was a long time ago, I said. No. I don't think of her. Not really. No.

You're never angry with her?

No, Kostya. I'm not.

He considered this. I wasn't sure if he believed me. It didn't matter. He caught me looking again at the photo.

We used to always wonder where you ran off to, Kostya said. You and your private life. Your imagined worlds.

I told him he was the one who had always wandered off. Him and his books.

He didn't respond to this. On the television a goal was scored, and he watched the silent shouting, the running.

I miss the air, Kostya said. Do you know this feeling? You're living whatever day you're in and you suddenly feel a longing. As though there's been an absence in you all this time and you never knew. But you don't know what it is. You can't find it. And it eats at you. For days it eats at you. Do you know it? I think I was missing the air. The takeoff. The first bank you make, the first turn. The world tilts, you look down. And then you go higher. I was missing that. I think that was what it must have been. Because I don't feel it when I'm up there. I feel, instead, held.

Kostya wasn't paying attention to the game anymore. He had picked up a pen. I watched as he leaned forward and colored in an old scratch on the desk.

You used to look for the bodies, he said. The victims of the camp. Do you remember? You were very young. It was before your father told you where the island was. And about coasts and oceans. You used to think the island was here. You would carry a shovel around, digging. Convinced you were living among ghosts. And I followed you. I helped . . .

I helped until the day my father caught us. But he couldn't

hit you. You see, Misha, there was your limp already. He felt sorry. We all did. So he went after me. He took your shovel and he went after me. And as he approached I thought he would strike my face. What surprised me was that he didn't. He hit my stomach. The way you would use a bayonet. The tip of the shovel ripped me open, and I think he would have pushed harder if he didn't wake from wherever he was . . .

When I think of that day it's never the pain or what happened or what we were doing or the shovel or even how young we were. I think of where my father was in that moment. Where in his mind he had gone. I had never seen that from him before and I never did again.

Kostya put down the pen. We heard the floor creak upstairs. I thought my father must be awake.

I said, I'll go get him.

Tomorrow, Kostya said. I'll see him tomorrow.

I reached over him and selected the first key I could from the wall. I placed it in his hand. I was standing behind Kostya now and I wrapped my arms around him and rested my chin on top of his head. I smelled the earth in his hair. He smiled again, jangling the keys.

What's the rate? he said.

On the house, I said.

On the house, he repeated.

That night Kostya slept in a room on the top floor. I brought him up. The rooms were all clean and the beds made. As I shut the door, I could see him sitting on the edge of the bed with his back to me. In the hallway I passed the faded botany drawings my father had purchased a long time ago.

I went down one floor. My father's room faced the street, above the reception. Mine was on the ground floor and he stayed up here. He liked being slightly above. His room was decorated identically to the others. He always said that if it was good enough for the guests, it was good enough for him.

I had been wrong earlier. I must have heard something else. I opened his door to check on him and he was asleep in the dark. His body and his blanket illuminated by the hallway. I was about to step out but he heard me and woke.

Misha, he said. Is everything all right?

I could hear the pull of a dream in his voice. I stepped in. I sat next to him. He turned on the bedside lamp.

He repeated what he had said, and I smiled. I said, Yes, yes, everything is fine.

I wanted to say that Kostya was here. But I kept myself from telling him for a little while longer.

I just wanted to be with him. I reached for his hands. I settled them onto my lap. His knuckles were cracked and dry. His lips were dry, too. I looked at his face. At his tired face that smelled of sleep and was speckled with moles, and I brushed back his gray hair.

I asked whether he had taken some aspirin. For his hands. But he was falling asleep again. He was shutting his eyes. He said, Misha, it's going to snow. Not tomorrow, but soon. Don't forget the spikes for your boots.

His grip on me loosened. Outside the window the boy passed again on his bicycle. I could hear the spin of the wheels. Then I heard the light turn off above me. I wondered where the moon went. And then there was nothing, only the buildings of this town and all the mountains.

Kostya stayed with us for a little while. In the mornings he would walk with me to the maintenance station. I thought he could work with me this time but he never went in, only waved. That's okay, Misha, he said. Have a good day. And then he walked back to the inn, where I would find him in the evenings.

I liked looking at them through the window, Kostya and my father sitting near the floor lamp, the two of them tracing the arc of something in the air, talking.

It's good now that you're here, my father often said to him, taking his hand.

And it was. For a time it was the way our lives had once

been. And I thought it would go on like this, the three of us together at the inn, not minding so much that there were no guests anymore, not minding the silences.

But as the months went on we began to see less of him. He wouldn't say where he went or what he did. He would return late or not return until days later, avoiding us. And then, like before, we didn't see him at all.

I went to the air base a few times. I stood at the gate and asked the guard whether Kostya was here but he wouldn't say. The guard was only a boy. He went back to reading his magazine. When I didn't leave, more guards came and took my arms and my shoulders, and they led me back to the road. One of them was older and recognized me. He knew I always failed the exams, and he told the other guards.

He said, Friend, you can't fly with that leg, and as they went back in he said something about the inn, something I couldn't hear from the road.

I walked to the field where I had first seen Kostya. I waited at the lake. I waited by the canoe, listening to the kids having their parties in the old homes. I kept looking up, for the airplanes. Then, one day, I stopped looking.

Winter started. It began to snow. The snow settled and didn't go away. I put spikes on the soles of my boots and a liner in my coat. I went to work and brought dinner home from the grocery store.

One night, replacing the chairs of a train car, I fell asleep. When I woke my left hand was in a bowl of warm water and two conductors were sitting beside me, grinning.

It didn't work, they said.

Misha, they said. You were supposed to piss your pants.

I waited for my eyes to adjust. It was bright, daytime. I saw the blue of their uniforms and then I looked out the car window. I focused on the great pale arches of a building looming over the tracks. I wasn't sure where I was.

Vladivostok Station, they said.

I sat up, awake. I moved too quickly and felt a muscle in my leg tighten and pull. I knocked the water over. They laughed. They rose and helped me up. One of them took out his handkerchief and wiped my hand. Then whatever mischief escaped from them, and they looked at me with a tenderness I hadn't seen in them before.

Misha, they said. We didn't want to wake you. You have an hour before we go back. It will be the local. Get some air, Misha. See the city. Have a coffee. Go shopping. Go find a woman.

They hit my shoulder.

Go, they said.

I stepped out onto the platform.

Just don't miss the train! they shouted, and laughed some more.

I entered the station. I passed through the waiting room where there was a mural on the ceiling of a skyline. I passed the chandeliers, the arched windows. Passengers were already waiting on the blue chairs for their trains.

I hadn't been here since my mother had taken me. We would come twice a year to shop. She was a city person, had always preferred it to where she was. The city was where she bought my father clothes. School supplies. Coloring books. And then the secret gifts. A small perfume for herself. Candy for me. I used to watch the way she would dip the bottle against one wrist, her arms suddenly alive with the smell of flowers and herbs. I would lean against her on the train ride back.

Where did she go? We never knew. Or if my father knew he never said. But I didn't think he did. I used to imagine her here alone, waiting for wherever she was going. In the room with the mural and the chandeliers. On the train platform. Wearing her long coat. My mother, Lidia, at the Vladivostok Station.

I went out into the city. I crossed the main road and headed toward the port. I stopped at a café and had a coffee. The woman behind the bar noticed my railway uniform under my coat and she gave the coffee to me for free.

In the distance, cargo was being loaded onto a ship, the arm of the crane pivoting in the gray sky. It was warmer here than in the mountains but still cold, the rain gutters and the edges of roofs already cluttered with icicles that would last and grow for months.

It was then I saw a bookshop. It was near the water, on a street corner. I approached the windows first, seeing what books they had on display. I thought that in another life I would like to make book covers. I didn't know whether that was something one could do for the rest of their lives, just that today, this morning, it made me happy thinking of it.

I had time. I went inside. The man behind the desk greeted me. I browsed the shelves. I saw novels and history books and books filled with poems. I wanted to buy one. I checked my pocket and realized my wallet was in my bag, which I had forgotten in the train car. I had only a few coins, not enough. I promised myself that I would come back one day and buy a book.

I returned to the street and approached the harbor. The sound of the ships and the machines grew louder. The birds. I could smell fish. Engine oil. A vendor was selling peanuts on the small boardwalk, the steam rising into the air. I walked to the first pier and back. I saw dockworkers in their thick gloves, their faces covered in masks to keep warm. I saw a ship with Japanese characters painted on its hull.

There was a telephone booth at the end. I slipped inside. Flyers with naked women were scattered on the floor. I took out the coins, pushed all of them in, and dialed. The glass of the booth was dirty and already fogging with my breath. I wiped the glass, revealing the harbor.

I didn't know if he would pick up. It kept ringing. I wondered if he was still asleep. Or if he had gone somewhere. I wondered where he might have gone. Where we would go.

A train whistled.

And then he was there. He picked up.

I held the telephone and looked out.

Dad, I said. I'm by the sea.

THE MOUNTAIN

I.

She had been at the stop since before the morning. She was often there, sitting on the bench, avoiding the rain. If she had enough coins she bought tea from the vending machine. If she didn't she waited to see if someone would give her some coins. She had nowhere to go. She stayed until someone noticed or until it got too dark or when, on a rare summer night, it got too cold. Even then she stayed a little longer, leaning into the hum of the vending machine, the brief air of a bus's open door.

One day a young man approached her about a job. He had been watching as all the buses picked up and dropped off passengers while she stayed, the tips of her shoes drenched by the spray of the tires. In her years in South Korea she had never been approached about anything except by men who asked her if she was lonely and wanted company. She felt the small knuckle of the pocketknife in her boot as he approached. She started to lean down but changed her mind. He waved a piece of paper at her in a way that reminded her of a long-ago friend whose face she could no longer recall, only that gesture, a wave before they went swimming.

He was wearing sunglasses even though there was no sun that day. He was young and handsome and smelled like an expensive fragrance. He also had on the sneakers she saw on the television at an electronics store downtown. A music video with dancers. A good song. She tapped her foot to the remembered beat as he stood at a respectful distance and opened the paper, which was a pamphlet, and showed her photos of an apartment complex. A great river. Parks.

Then he spoke in Mandarin, which surprised her. She spoke in Mandarin back to him. She said she liked his sunglasses.

He laughed and bought her tea. He sat down. A puddle began to form on the uneven road, catching a portion of the sky. He said it was okay if she no longer had her documents. He said they would take care of her. On the back of the pamphlet was the name of a ferryboat and a pier number in the harbor. Below that was written a time and day.

She looked away to cough and wiped her mouth, swallowing some phlegm she would spit out if he weren't here.

Come back home, he said.

He didn't wait for her to answer. A bus pulled up and she watched him get on, still stunned by what he said, still confused. She wondered if he meant the city. She looked down at the pamphlet, searching the photos, not yet recognizing the river. Then she did and even though she knew the stranger was gone she leaned forward to follow the route of the bus as it made its way down the hill.

She wondered if they had met in an old life. He wasn't the friend she used to swim with, she knew that, but she wondered all the same if this man knew her in some way, had known all of them who used to swim there, waiting for their fathers. Where were all of them now? It felt as though she hadn't thought of them in years. She tried again to place the man she had just met, tried again to place him in that river.

It was only after the bus vanished from her view that she noticed the sunglasses. They lay on the bench beside her. They were like the ones from the movie about the American Navy. She left them alone, counting the raindrops falling against the plastic shelter above her. She watched the surface of the puddle as it kept breaking. She coughed again and spat out her phlegm. The advertisement screen switched from an energy drink to the new camera she had begun to see on the streets and the boardwalks. Anyone who could afford it was buying one.

She finished her tea and then put the sunglasses on. There was a nice weight to them.

Her name was Faye. She was twenty-six. She had been in South Korea for over ten years. She was in the port city of Incheon and she could see the harbor from the stop.

In the puddle, two birds moved from one level of sky to another.

She thought she would see the man again but she didn't. She took the ferryboat with six others and entered the sea. She thought they would leave in the dark or that they would be hidden somewhere far below the deck, the way she had come years ago, but neither happened. They left in the bright of day, the captain and the four crew members wearing shirts that advertised a tour group—*Sunshine Tours*—and one even had a loudspeaker and began to talk about Incheon during the war.

There were more women than men on board. Most of them spoke Mandarin though there was a Korean man and a Russian. Some were bored by the slow trip; others were eager or anxious. There were two women who whispered often to each other. They were frightened as the coastline vanished and the hours passed. Frightened because it might not be a factory they would be working at. Or an apartment building they would be living in. That they had been tricked like so many others. It must have occurred to them before they had agreed to come and yet they had come to the dock just like Faye.

It had of course occurred to her. That all of this was something else. But she still boarded. She boarded after studying the photos. She had slipped her father's pocketknife into her underwear as she walked across the gangplank but they didn't check her body or even her bag. On the ferryboat the closest anyone ever got to her was when they passed out water bottles. Or helped them hours later as they switched vessels far at sea.

On the new boat, as the day ended, they listened to a crew member repeat a few Mandarin phrases for the ones who didn't speak the language. All the passengers took turns saying them. Even Faye, who hadn't spoken certain phrases in a long time. She felt her tongue loosen. A familiar turn of her mouth and her voice. A slipping into years she had stopped thinking of.

They were given a dinner of gel packets. The gel came in a foil pack the size of a playing card you tore at the corner and sucked on. The shelters carried them and so did the vending machine at the bus stop. She chose the shrimp-flavored one. Her father would have liked the sweet potato.

She kept the sunglasses on. She thought of the young man and his friendliness and wondered if it was sincere or whether talking to people like her was something he did. She knew it was the latter but wondered all the same.

It was a larger boat and to keep active they were encouraged to pace the deck. She walked back and forth as the sun was setting. She never saw the ocean that first time, leaving, hidden below the deck. Now she was embraced by a vastness she hadn't imagined. It covered her. It left her breathless and distracted.

The crew members appeared. They gathered at the center of the deck in a circle and huddled together. With their bodies leaning toward each other they resembled a tree. Or a closed flower. She recalled the strange tree from when she was younger, bone white and disfigured. How they had found her father collapsed there. Where had that been? Where was that tree? A field. The low sun on him. That river.

The crew members were still huddled together. Then

they all leaned back suddenly and looked up. She saw an arm lift, a palm open, and a metallic ball flew above their heads and hovered for a moment before it shot up into the air. It flew in silence. Or if there was a noise she couldn't hear it. Only this thing the size of a child's fist shooting straight up into the sky and vanishing.

It returned a few minutes later. It drifted down, touching the hand that sent it up. She could now see the bracelet the man was wearing and the ball landed on that. She heard a click and a whirring. Everyone on deck gathered as the man tapped on the bracelet and from the ball a video of the sea projected into the air. The image was colorful and textured, their boat the size of a thumbnail, the fading wake.

It could have gone higher, she heard one of the crew members say.

It's still cool, someone else said.

Faye walked closer. As the video zoomed in on the boat she recognized her own shape on the deck. The top of her head. Her arms and her hands. The other passengers as well, all from above and scattered. Then the video tilted and caught the sun moving down past the horizon.

Faye looked out across the ocean, the sun now gone, only the remaining light.

She asked the men where in the ocean they were but they couldn't tell her that. They seemed disappointed in her in some way she didn't understand. They turned the camera off and dispersed. The passengers continued on their walks around the deck. The Russian practiced Mandarin.

It was summer. Faye returned to the railing. She caught the first stars. The sudden moon.

She had only wanted to remember. And come back.

In the morning they entered a quiet bay somewhere south of Lianyungang. She could see fishing huts behind a copse and rafts on the sand. The smell of a grill made her mouth water. They disembarked onto a small motorboat, three at a time, and climbed the beach toward a van that was waiting for them. The driver said something she couldn't hear and pulled opened the side door.

Faye was the last to get in. As she watched the boat turn and motor away, she was struck by a sudden hollowing, as though her chest was caving in. As though there was a core part of her that was still far at sea. Why had she come back? She was no longer sure. A dull pain rose from her side. She rubbed the space and coughed, swallowing the phlegm. She looked around at the beach and the huts. Two children wearing shirts but no pants were looking back. She heard the flap of their sandals as they jumped on a log and regained their balance.

She felt a hand on her arm. One of the women from the boat was reaching down. The woman didn't appear to be frightened anymore. She was a little older than Faye and said, Come on, and Faye climbed into the van.

They drove for many hours. They drove without stopping. If one of them had to use the bathroom the others turned and pretended to ignore the sound of piss hitting the bucket. The only windows in the back of the van were on the rear doors, so whatever Faye saw of the road and the landscape was as it was pulling away.

They were heading south into Shanghai. It was where she was born, where her father had been born and where they had once lived, the two of them, first in the city and then farther out, closer to the chemical plant, Faye always at home and her father at work. Faye's mother left them a long time ago.

The driver turned on the radio and they listened to pop songs. Some of them were K-pop, and the Korean man sang along holding an imaginary microphone. He claimed to be a karaoke champion, which made some of them laugh, even though they couldn't deny his voice was beautiful. Deep and lulling, like the water on some days.

She would never know his name but she would always remember him, even much later, when her life and her days were so far from how she ever imagined them. For his singing that calmed her while she gazed out the window, where there was the country that used to be her home, receding, where there was nothing familiar on that first day, not even the trees and the different-colored fields, the horses and the river, road signs and businesses, fluorescent lights still on in the daytime.

II.

They never told her what part of the camera she would put together. That first day she was brought to the factory, was given a uniform, and sent to the production floor. She hadn't slept. She followed a woman to a track. A siren blared; the belt began to move, and blue bins appeared. She watched as the woman beside her picked up a small pin and inserted it into a chamber. That was all. Every day a pin and a chamber.

At first she hurried. Then the woman told her to slow.

It's okay, the woman said. They don't want your hands to cramp.

She spoke from behind her mask. They were all wearing

masks. And hairnets and eyeglasses and gloves and aprons. She had yet to see the woman's face. The woman had yet to see hers. She heard someone across the track complain about the mask but Faye didn't mind. She liked the anonymity of it, of not knowing who was working beside her.

She assembled the parts all morning. No one spoke. On occasion the floor manager checked on them, tapping on a tablet, and the woman beside Faye looked up at him whenever he came close, but for most of the hours they were left alone.

It was a vast space, with different sections, sections she would never visit or see, with different belts and machines. Above her hung a galaxy of lightbulbs. All around them were high, narrow windows, too narrow to see anything outside, though there was the occasional shadow, the shifting daylight. She grew used to the steady whir and the hum of gears, the track belts and the robotic arms. Sometimes a door at the far end opened and workers exited, pushing carts with white boxes wrapped in cellophane.

It was the cleanest place Faye had ever worked. It smelled of nothing. The air cool and pleasant on her neck and her wrists. The sun went down a bit and she found herself standing on her toes, hoping to catch its path.

Earlier that day they had gone to the apartment complex.

It wasn't like the photo in the pamphlet at all. It was tall and wide, made of concrete, and was farther up the river, on the border to a forest. There were outdoor corridors on each floor like at the motel where she once worked, cleaning the rooms, pocketing the small bottles of shampoo. Sometimes she stole naps on the motel beds, watching the ceiling fans spin, the shadows of the blades moving across a wall light and a painting.

Those paintings. They were always of the sea.

She had only one bottle left of the shampoo.

The morning shift ended. There was a vending machine in the locker room. They had been given some coins and Faye bought a gel pack. She took off her mask. The woman who had been working alongside her took off her mask, too. She was pretty and a few years older than Faye. Her name was Yonha and she was Korean and they sat on the bench in front of their lockers and they ate and talked a little about themselves.

Yonha started working at the factory six months ago. Before this she had been in the city. Faye said she came from South Korea and they talked about that, too.

Faye asked if she lived in the complex. Yonha laughed.

Yes, she said, Of course. Everyone does. I'm on the floor above, the seventh. You'll hear roller skates. All morning and night. My daughter. As though she owns no shoes.

Yonha bought another gel pack.

Do you party? Yonha asked.

Sure.

Yonha said it was better here. The city was better here. The men were better here. Yonha said this and laughed again. Faye liked her laugh. Her ease. Yonha sucked on her gel pack and said she liked Faye's name. Was it an American name? She wished she had an American name.

Faye wasn't sure. She nodded anyway, not wanting to disappoint her. She was named after an actress in a gangster movie whose title she couldn't remember, the one her mother liked to watch while she got stoned. It was dubbed, so Faye never knew what language the actors were speaking, whether it was English or some other language she didn't know.

The food made her sleepy. Sleepy from the journey. The day. The production line. She looked around and searched for the others who came with her but couldn't find anyone. She rubbed her side. She coughed.

They heard a whistle. Next shift.

She watched Yonha put up her hair. She noticed a tattoo behind the woman's ear. She wondered if her daughter looked like her. And what she was like.

They got back to the floor. The siren blared and they got a

new bin. From behind their masks they looked at each other and began to work again.

All that week it was the same. They took the bus down the river road, checked in with the security guards at the gates, changed, waited for the bins. She and Yonha shared a locker. Some days they stood beside each other; others days the floor manager came in and sent Yonha somewhere else.

She bought gel packs from the vending machine. She worked all day. At the end of the shift she waited in line for the X-ray machine and the scanners to move up and down. None of the guards were ever there, only a security camera in the high corner. Once, when no one was behind her, she peeked at the screen, thinking she would see her skeleton. But there was only the heat of her, in layers, like the weather maps she saw on the channel her father used to watch, the pale storms pulsing, aswirl.

It took her a moment to get used to the outside. To get used to the sun if there was sun. Rain if there was rain. Smog from the city. Air. For her eyes to adjust to the late day, the remaining light. She felt a hand slip under her arm. Yonha pulled her across the lot, waving to the guards and their floor manager, and they crossed the street toward the bus stop. In the distance, far beyond the road, were the skyscrapers of the city defining the horizon. As a child she had only spent a few years there. She wondered if it was all the same or whether it would be unrecognizable if she ever went back.

The bus was always full. Yonha sat on her lap. She smelled like almond soap. She wanted to ask where she got her soap but grew shy. She held Yonha and watched the river as they headed toward the complex. There were boats pulling cargo. Benches holding couples and their private happiness. The distant hills. Workers used to call this river Factory Row. Her father had worked at the chemical plant farther down, deep in the country.

She still thought of the man who sat with her on the bench. She still wondered if she would see him again. Yonha had liked the sunglasses, too. When they were dropped off at the complex Yonha took them from her and danced in the playground near the river, humming a song. Someone had gathered old tires to build a fortress. Yonha climbed them and shouted up at the men looking down from the apartment balconies. She was asking them for money so they could head to the city nightclubs.

It grew dark. The skyscrapers in the city grew brighter. The apartment complex, too, tall above them with all the windows and the outdoor corridors, some lined with old, blinking Christmas lights. She could make out clotheslines. Curtains of beads hanging on some entrances.

Faye watched as a child, a girl, appeared on the playground, roller-skating. It was Yonha's daughter. They had yet to meet. She was seven, Faye thought. She looked at her mother still on the tire fortress but didn't stop and skated up the river road. When an old woman appeared, pushing a cart, the child stopped and waited for the woman to pass. The cart was full of house supplies and clothes and she was calling out to the building, wondering if anyone needed anything. Faye saw someone on the first floor call her over. She saw the old woman lift a pair of sneakers with blinking lights on the soles, streaks of blue in the air.

Yonha's daughter kept going. Faye had an urge to follow her but Yonha, still wearing the sunglasses, jumped down from the tires, took her hands, and they ended up dancing together in the playground. Then she let go of Faye and danced up the stairs of the complex, leaving her there.

Faye had trouble sleeping that night. She wasn't used to having her own room. She couldn't remember the last time she had slept in one. The last time she had one to herself. In South Korea, there were the shelters and the riverbanks and the bridges but this was a room, a narrow single room with a lightbulb on the ceiling and one bare window that faced the outdoor corridor. The size of a storage shed. Still it was hers.

Life seemed simple here: they worked, they were given coins for meals, they were given a room. When they arrived the van driver had told them they were happy to find somewhere else. No one had left. But she didn't know where they were now, what floor. She had yet to see any of them again, unaware that most of them she would never see again in the vastness of the complex and the rhythm of their new days.

Her first night she had opened the door to find litter scattered all across the floor. Stale air. Dusty blankets. She had pushed everything to a corner, too tired to do anything else, but the next day she borrowed a broom from Yonha and swept. She picked up a crushed, empty pack of cigarettes. Chocolate wrappers and a porn magazine. Newspapers. She banged out dust from the blankets and used them as a bed. She threw everything away except the newspapers and the porno, hiding them under the blankets.

She tried to imagine who it was that had been here before. Why they left. If anyone in the building noticed them gone. She traced the holes in the wooden wall beside her where someone must have pinned something. She had once stayed in a room behind a noodle shop. Every night the owner left her Styrofoam containers of leftover soup. To her, warmth in the winter was forever the smell of broth, chicken, barley, and kelp.

This was home now. How long she would be here? She always wondered that wherever she was. And what did she have? There were some clothes she kept in her bag. Money now from the factory. A stack of Styrofoam cups from the noodle shop. Her last bottle of shampoo from the motel.

She had been here before. This part of the river. This piece of land. She had walked by here when there wasn't an apartment building. She picked up the newspapers and read the dates on them. The headlines. She was orienting herself again. She thought it would feel different. She didn't know what it was she was feeling. She was tired. Tired from the factory. Still tired from the journey. The years. But she couldn't sleep. She coughed and rubbed her side. She missed swimming.

At the chemical plant, they were never warned to avoid the water. So they all used to swim the river. The parents taking their children. Her father finding her there after his shift and joining her, leaping. Across the road, the plant owner would get into his car and drive away.

Her father. She used to boil rice and try to feed him as he died. She would bathe his body with his own shirt, soaking it in the sink. Never tall or strong enough to help him cross the room. Her father who loved to swim. To meet her there in the water.

She thought she heard the faint noise of roller skates. She flipped through the porno. The pictures were faded. Some of them were torn, their heads missing so that there were only bodies. The faint shadows of characters. She wondered if she threw away the missing heads when she was cleaning the room.

She thought of the field with the strange tree. A tree and horses. She listened to the people next door arguing. Then someone appeared by her window. And someone else. She hadn't yet gotten blinds and they looked in and moved on.

One day, after work, Faye heard a knock on her door. She thought it was Yonha. But when she peered around the blanket she had hung up she saw the Karaoke Champion standing there. She hadn't seen him since the van ride. The light in the corridor had gone out, so he was just a silhouette as he walked in.

She had been asleep. She yawned. She lay down. He crawled on top of her, pausing for a moment to look down at the magazine she had been flipping through earlier, study-ing the headless women. He moved his hands over her, up her stomach to her breasts. She lay there and let him but he stopped. She heard him groan. She thought he stopped because of the magazine. Or because she hadn't reacted. She said it was okay if he went on but he groaned again and moved away and sat against the wall across from her. He sighed. He stretched out his legs. He wasn't wearing shoes and his bare feet touched hers.

You're alone, he said.

Faye sat up. They were in the dark.

I have four others, he said. In my room. You're alone.

I think so, she said. So far.

She could feel his moving toes. They were at first cold and then warm. It felt good, like the soft touch of a hand. She pressed her own feet against his.

A spotlight turned on in the distance. The beam rotated in the sky. It touched the wall and him and then she saw the bruises all over his face. She held her breath. Her hands tightened. He was drooling blood. It kept dripping and he caught it in his palm and brought it up to his mouth as though not wanting to stain her floor. Or not wanting anything else to leave him. She looked down at her own shirt and saw a splatter of blood there, too. She hadn't felt it.

Come here, he said.

She slid over beside him so that they were both leaning against the wall, looking up at a corner of the window. She heard roller skates tumble by. A far song.

Do you know the first traveler? Karaoke Champion said.

He was having trouble speaking but still he talked, and she leaned against his shoulder, wondering if the touching hurt.

He said the first traveler had large hands. That every year the man would rest somewhere and open them and from those hands his children were born. But the traveler was afraid of water, so he caught the children before they fell, placing them on his shoulders, where they were forced to live, forbidden from ever coming down. So the children stayed up there, peering down at the oceans and the rivers. They saw their own faces reflected below. They waved and from across that distance their hands waved back. They sang and their songs formed the wind that broke their image.

But as the years went on their curiosity grew. And so one night, as the traveler slept, they snuck down. They entered a river. And the traveler woke from the sound of their bodies and their singing and he saw what they had done and, furious, he reached down and began to gather them, lifting them into the air by their hair and their limbs. He licked their hands and their feet. He bound them, child by child, forming arches, and he scattered those arches across the earth. Their laughter he used to light lanterns. Their sorrow turned their skin pale. Their eyes dulled, their songs faded.

Winter came. The spring. Then more years. The man

grew old. The lines on his palms vanished. New travelers came, crossing the first bridges.

Faye hadn't moved. She watched his toes curl.

I like the impossible stories, Karaoke Champion said.

He let go and struggled to stand, holding his bruised face. Faye tried to help but he waved her away. He approached the door.

I don't want to stay here anymore, he said, and stepped outside.

Faye followed him. All the way down and across the lawn. There was an umbrella someone had left on the playground and he paused, picked it up, and closed it. A power generator hummed. Karaoke Champion left the umbrella on the bench and walked down the river road, following the path of the streetlamps.

She didn't know if she would ever see him again. She was blinded momentarily by a scooter approaching the apartment complex. The floor manager was driving and Yonha was sitting behind him. Neither noticed Faye in the playground as they headed in. She had climbed the slide. She looked up as she slid down. Cigarette ash was falling from all the balconies.

At the end of her first week, someone stole Faye's bag from her room. There was money inside, some spare clothes, and her

Styrofoam cups. They left the blankets alone. Also, the clothes she wore that day, hanging on the wall. She thought the sunglasses were gone but remembered Yonha had borrowed them.

She had forgotten to lock her door. She had gone to the showers. Gripping her father's pocketknife, she stayed under the water, massaging the side of her stomach.

As Faye returned down the corridor, a small camera almost hit her as it flew by and out toward the country. She leaned over the railing, saw two children controlling it from the playground. She followed the camera's path into the growing dark, farther up the river, where the chemical plant used to be. She had yet to ask anyone if it was still there. She was about to call down to the children, wanting to know what they were recording, but grew shy.

Wrapped in her towel, unaware her door was ajar, Faye stayed by the rail, waiting for the camera to come back from the distance.

III.

There was a party at the apartment complex. It was a Friday and some women were hosting. They changed into their party clothes after their shift. They thought it would be more fun that way. They sat on the benches and put on makeup in front of their lockers, taking turns holding up a mirror for each other.

Faye didn't know about the party and hadn't brought any clothes with her. She didn't own party clothes. She didn't own makeup either. She didn't think she would go. She had vomited in the morning and hadn't eaten.

Yonha sat down and opened her lipstick. Hold still, Yonha said, and painted Faye's lips, and then told her not to blink and pulled on her lashes with mascara. Faye was holding the mirror. She didn't know why but she was avoiding her own eyes. She looked down at the reflection of her lips instead, bright pink. She tilted the mirror up and caught, through a narrow window, the moon. Yonha told Faye to open her mouth. Faye thought it was more lipstick but Yonha placed a pill on her tongue.

It won't make you hungry anymore, Yonha said.

They joined the others and moved through the X-ray machines. They waved to the guards. They crossed the street to the bus stop and when it came they went to the back, sharing a row, being loud, an older woman turning and Yonha sticking out her tongue. Above the windows were advertisements for the new model of the camera they assembled every day. It was just the small sphere against a blue background, like the sky. Perhaps it was the sky.

She didn't know what Yonha had given her. She waited for her body to feel different in some way, or her vision, but nothing happened. She massaged her side and watched a boat pulling cargo inland. For a while the bus kept pace with it until the road elevated and the boat disappeared. They stopped at other factories to let people off and they headed out into the country, past the farms. The fields turned into large lots where there were the apartment complexes.

The other women all lived on the eighth floor. They had taken the floor over for the evening. They had hung lights. They opened the doors to their rooms and brought out speakers so that the corridor was filled with music. It was already crowded. She wasn't sure if it was the pill or the music or the crowd but she felt a hovering lightness and let go of Yonha's hand, losing her.

Faye lost all of them, moving across the floor that looked like the other floors as everyone danced. She felt a body brush up against hers. Another. Her own body swayed. Her head bobbed. She didn't feel sick anymore. She didn't feel tired anymore. She wasn't hungry. A camera flew over them, in the air. Or she thought it was a camera, it was hard to tell. Someone was twirling a string of colored lights over the balcony. She heard singing. She recognized the voice. She clung to it as she wove her way through the corridor and kept looking. Her body was all air. She couldn't stop swaying. She reached the end but there was no one.

A door was open to one of the rooms. She walked in and found Yonha with their floor manager from the factory. They were half dressed and their limbs were wrapped around each other. Faye's sunglasses were on the ground beside them. They didn't notice as she picked them up and put them on.

Where's the Karaoke Champion? she said, returning to the corridor, though no one answered.

She kept moving. She walked down past the twirling lights and she didn't remember heading down the stairs but she was suddenly on a different floor. There were dancers here, too, and music. She caught the familiar K-pop song again and bobbed her head and watched as two young boys took turns wearing a bracelet and controlling a camera she couldn't see in the dark over the balconies. She leaned over the rail. She saw someone below. She kept heading down. Floor by floor.

Outside, she found Yonha's daughter in the playground.

Hey! Faye called. The girl turned. Have you seen the Karaoke Champion?

Yonha's daughter hesitated, studying Faye as she approached.

Please, Faye said. Don't go. I know your mother.

The girl skated away.

Faye walked to the road. The party music followed her, another song. Someone was still twirling lights in the air high above on the eighth floor. She winced. The pain had returned on her side. She felt around and pressed against it. She grew dizzy and approached the river, wanting to go farther away.

I promise I'll come back, she said, not realizing she said it out loud.

On the bank she fell to her knees and vomited. She shivered. There was a tightness in her chest. She punched the ground with her hands. She breathed and waited. She felt better but she was freezing. She was thirsty. She searched the debris on the bank. She crawled closer to the water but heard a car.

It was a pickup truck. The truck slowed as she stepped out. There was a group on the flatbed and they were wearing dresses and tuxedos and party masks. The masks had briefly frightened her but she kept staring up at them. At the way they were all gathered closely together on the flatbed. The glitter that sparkled in the moonlight.

One of the women reached down. She reached down with a gentleness that reminded Faye of an arm underwater, the completion of a stroke.

Do you know the Karaoke Champion? Faye asked her.

The woman smiled. She touched Faye's hand.

There's a better party, the woman said.

The truck drove farther into the country. The farther they went the less she felt the drug. She thought she had vomited out most of it. She was awake and no longer shivering. She had forgotten she was still wearing the sunglasses. She pushed them up. There were no streetlamps here. There was a hush in the wind. In the people, too, wearing their tuxedos and dresses and masks, all of them looking up at the clear sky.

They said it was more rare now, for the sky to be so clear. They said tomorrow or the next day there would be smog in the air. All day, the smog. They drove on, following the river. They passed an old farm. A silo. The hills and the first mountains.

She didn't know what time it was but now her mind felt clear. Clearer than most days. She lifted her arm and saw the night on her skin. The hairs on her arms. They were approaching an old wooden sign near the riverbank and that was when she remembered. She stood quickly. She felt one of the men take hold of her wrist to steady her as the truck shook.

Stop, Faye said. Stop the truck. We're here.

We know, the man said, and she looked down at him, confused.

The truck slowed. It turned down a dirt road near the river and the man let go. She jumped off. The men and the women in their masks looked back at her as they entered the woods. She went back across the main road. She was facing the river and beyond that a high mountain.

That was where she swam, waiting for her father to finish his shift. She and the other children, all of them swimming.

Here was where her father worked.

She returned into the woods where the truck had gone. The farther she went she could smell garbage. She had been to the chemical plant only a few times but she could see it in her mind now. When she reached the road's end, though, there was nothing. There was the truck already parked by an old chain-link fence and beyond that a landfill. Hills of garbage. The stench. Someone had cut a hole in the fence. Faye covered her face with her hands and went in.

The buildings were gone. In the dark, she could see no evidence of the chemical plant. She walked around, weaving through the mounds of garbage. She wondered where her father had worked, whether she was walking over it now, his floor, his locker. On occasion she caught a reflection: glass, perhaps, tin. She couldn't get used to the smell.

She heard voices. Or she thought they were voices. She stopped and waited. Through the canopy the sky cleared and then clouded. She heard the sounds again and rounded a bend. Up ahead a halo of bare lightbulbs hung in the air above a clearing. Below that was a roped-in ring. A small crowd had formed around the perimeter. She went down the slope.

Faye approached the crowd, which was small, intimate. Two dozen. The men and the women from the truck were there, too, though they had taken off their masks, lit cigars, and undid their bow ties. They were all watching two men in the small, roped-in ring. Faye stayed in the periphery, listening to that new sound of skin hitting and breaking skin. Unable to move, she watched the fighters fall and fall again.

She caught the face of one of them and moved closer. She moved to the front.

It was the young man who had approached her on the bench in Incheon. The one who had convinced her to come. He fell and she watched as he struggled to find some energy in a far part of him and get up and then he charged and pinned his opponent to the ground. In the dust lifting around them, he began to strike. She saw the brief flash of pain in his face as his knuckles connected with his opponent's nose but he did it again, she heard a crack, and that was all she saw.

Two men stepped in front of her, blocking her view. She didn't move. She didn't know what happened. She didn't move but listened, trying to follow the orchestra of his movements until there was clapping.

There were more fights. Other fighters. She stayed in that spot the whole time. All the rest of the night. Until all the fighting stopped and the crowd dispersed. She waited for everyone to go. The people from the truck walked by, one of them slipping his bow tie over her neck. It smelled of cigars.

She found the man from the bus stop later, off to the side, beyond the rim of the lightbulbs. He was lying in the dirt with his eyes closed. He had fallen asleep. She almost couldn't recognize him. One of his eyes was bloated and there were cuts on his lips and the skin over the bridge of his nose had split. She knelt down. Sat with him. She lifted his head as gently as she could and settled it on her lap.

The sky was lightening. There was the blue. The last stars. She began to shiver again. She felt the cold air on her back as she held him, feeling his warmth. His blood. She combed his hair with her hands.

He woke and looked up from her lap. He smiled.

Those are mine, he said, and tried to lift his hand toward the sunglasses on her head. He winced. He almost cried. His right hand was broken. It lay there dead on his chest. He was still looking at her.

You don't look well, he said.

She laughed. No?

He smiled again.

This is nice, he said, and shut his eyes, settling into her.

Is this what you do? she said.

No, he said. Not really. No. I bring people here. For this. The fights.

She was trying to understand. He was drifting, losing the thread. He opened his eyes again, or tried to, and searched for his cigarettes. She lit one for him and they shared it.

I just wanted, he said. I just wanted to know. What it was like. To be in there.

He faced the empty ring. He looked across at it for a while, as though some part of him was still there, as though he were pulling that part back into him.

So you bring people like that, she said. And you bring people like me.

People like you, he repeated, as though holding those words in his mouth.

You never told me your name.

Tad, he said. I'm Tad.

Faye and Tad, she said. That sounds like a song.

A bad song, he said.

He lifted his other hand and tapped the bow tie around her neck.

What did you mean? Faye said. When we met. At the bus stop. When you said to come back home?

He frowned. He didn't remember saying that. He switched to Shanghainese.

Welcome home, he said.

Thank you, she said, and laughed again.

They were alone. She wasn't used to laughing. As he fell asleep on her lap she watched the light spread in the trees. The rope sway in the wind. She wrapped the bow tie around his hand. She slipped off the sunglasses and put them on him.

That day he stayed with her. She helped him to his scooter and she drove back down the river road. She left the scooter near the playground and brought him up. There were rem nants of the party. Hanging lights. Some doors open. They stepped over someone asleep in the corridor. She brought Tad to her room, settled him down, and she rushed back down, took the scooter, and drove to the factory.

She was late for her shift. The others had been working for an hour by the time she entered the production floor. The pain had returned in her side and she hurried, ignoring it.

The manager spotted her and yelled. He had never spoken to her before. He leaned in close and jabbed her in the chest. He did it in a way that didn't hurt but was insistent and soft, as though he were studying that small part of her near her breast.

Perhaps it was this or her exhaustion, or something else. She was unaware she was holding one of the pins that was supposed to go into a chamber. Every day a pin into a chamber. A blue bin. A small star of heat under her rib. In her mind she stepped back and pushed his hand away. She witnessed his eyes widen. His surprise.

She looked down and saw her hand gripping the pin and the pin deep in the manager's hand. She heard a scream. It wasn't him and it wasn't her. It was Yonha behind, who had come to help and Yonha saw the manager's hand and screamed. She called the manager by his name, the way she did whenever he came to visit her at the complex. She called his name and reached for him.

And this would always surprise Faye: the man hit Yonha first. For screaming. For calling him by his name. He struck her with his other hand and over the sound of the assembly lines she could hear the impact and Yonha stumbled to the floor. And as Faye turned the man hit her, too. He hit Faye a second time when she was on the floor and she felt the cold shock of her tooth entering the side of her mouth. She tasted her own blood.

Another manager rushed in. Some workers were watching but they returned to their lines. She looked up at the man-ager standing over them both and he ripped the pin out of his hand and dropped it. She heard the music of it hitting the floor and followed the line of blood flowing down his arm.

Lying there, still hearing the ringing of the pin, she waited for what would happen next. He could hit her again. He could call the police or other supervisors. She could be sent away. It occurred to her that she didn't care. If he hit her again. If she were sent away. Tomorrow she could get back on a boat and go. She could go anywhere. To that part of the sea she remembered. Somewhere else.

But the man wasn't looking at her. He was looking at Yonha. He sucked on the wound and kicked the pin toward them. He said, Put it back in the bin, and walked away.

She left early that day, alone, left the locker door open, and drove Tad's scooter back down the river road. At the com-plex she climbed up to the sixth floor as fast as she could. Yonha's daughter was in the corridor, roller-skating. The girl stopped, staring at her bruised face as Faye hurried into her room.

She thought at first he was there, in the pile of blankets. She tried to touch her jaw and then pressed her forehead against the wall. She held her stomach and vomited. She waited for the nausea to pass, her body still sore, her jaw tender and raw. She spat. Wiping her mouth, she noticed the girl standing by the open door.

You live here? Yonha's daughter said.

She was holding a Styrofoam cup and wearing a dress. It was a nice dress. Faye looked away, ashamed at the mess she made.

You should see a doctor, the girl said. You don't look so good.

I've been told that, Faye said.

It was the first time she had heard Yonha's daughter speak. She was speaking a dialect Faye hadn't heard since she was a child. Faye's mother's dialect. Yonha had never said where the girl was born. Who the father had been.

You know my mother? the girl said.

Yes, Faye said.

The man here said to tell you he had to go away for a while, the girl said. On business. He said you would know what he meant. He said to come tell you that. When you came.

The girl lifted her finger and tapped her own cheek.

He looked like that, too, she said.

Faye lowered her hands. She couldn't say why but she didn't mind Yonha's daughter staring at her bruised face but she didn't want the girl to see her touching her side. She wiped her mouth again. She asked if there was any water in that cup. The girl reached across and gave her the rest.

He said he would come back, the girl said. But not with people like you. Or, he said with people like you. I'm sorry. I can't remember anymore.

It's all right, Faye said.

Can I go? the girl said, tapping her skates on the wall.

You can go. Wait. Did you take my bag?

What?

Never mind. Tell me your name.

No, the girl said.

It hurt Faye to smile. She wasn't sure if she did.

Yonha's daughter skated down the corridor. Faye lay down. The door was still open. She thought the girl would pass by again but she didn't. There was just her shadow by the door and the sound of the wheels moving back and forth.

IV.

She stayed on at the factory. They didn't fire her or report her. They didn't report Yonha either. They kept working there together, though they no longer spoke often to each other.

Through the days the bruising on Yonha's face faded. Faye's diminished but it didn't entirely go away, even after her jaw healed. The bruise looked like a small ink stain on her cheek. In the locker room she changed as fast as she could and kept to herself most days.

One night before taking the bus, Yonha opened a compact and dabbed a sponge into it. She told Faye to hold still and powdered her cheek, masking the bruise. From then on, Yonha left the compact in their locker.

Summer was ending but the heat lingered for a little while longer. The smog in the air, too, which occurred once in a while, depending on the wind. It was heaviest on that Saturday. It started before the morning and came down low and it was impossible to see the top of the apartment complex. Faye had never seen it like this before. She walked out onto the corridor and saw nothing.

She hadn't heard from Tad but she still had his scooter. She had gotten good at driving it and once, when she was feeling better, she had gone to the landfill but he wasn't there. She went over to the wooden sign on the riverbank and sat on an old tree trunk, facing the high mountain, trying to remember. Twelve years ago. She wondered if that was a long time or not. She couldn't say. She was no longer sure what a long time meant, only that there were things she remembered and things she had forgotten and she didn't know why that happened.

The day of the heavy smog she drove into the city. She followed the road until it turned into a freeway. As soon as she entered the border she knew it was a different city then. There had been more space in the sky. But still she knew some of the roads. Those she remembered. And the districts. She drove until she reached the coast, skirting the downtown, winding around the skyscrapers that were hidden in the smog.

She arrived at a beach, parking near the boardwalk. It was worse here. There was no one. There was rope blocking the entrances, warning of the smog. A new hotel was nearby. Through a long window she could see the travelers and the tourists gathered in a restaurant. Some wore the kind of masks she wore at the factory.

Faye ducked under the rope. She headed down. She picked up a shell, holding it in her palm. She walked up the beach toward the hotel. Some people from the restaurant began to notice her. She turned and walked back. She couldn't see the city anymore. She approached the water. Took off her shoes. The water was warm and heavy. Slow. It slipped over her feet and the hem of her jeans. It retreated. She stepped in farther. She breathed. She clenched her hands and let go. She felt the water rise and retreat.

A man stepped out from the hotel. He was wearing a uniform and a mask. He approached her from the beach, swinging his arms, shouting at her to go back.

Faye left before he arrived.

She knew the roads and she knew the neighborhood but she couldn't remember the house. The one she was born in and the one she lived in before she moved closer to the chemical plant. She knew only that it was a lane house and they lived for five years on the third floor. Her mother was there for the first two. They had a small television. A brown corduroy couch. A painting above that her father had found in the alley trash container. Faye had gone with him. They pretended they had bought it together as a gift for Faye's mother. A birthday gift.

It was a painting of a mountain though where the mountain was they never knew. She never knew either whether her mother had believed them, that they had bought it at the market. She had no memory of her mother ever looking at it. Or what made her father lie. What made Faye join him in the story.

Faye's mother had been a maid. A hotel maid. She came home every day and microwaved ramen, watched dubbed movies on the television, and smoked.

Most days Faye sat on the balcony, behind the house-plant and the hanging laundry. There were other families on the floors below. Sometimes the neighbors would appear and Faye watched from above. The lane. The cats. The old woman who sat in front of the café and sold flowers. She was the oldest woman Faye knew and all day she sat in the same space as people passed through the lane and entered and left the café. On occasion they saw each other though they never acknowledged it. The old woman sold very few flowers and Faye wondered where all the others went. She wondered what else the woman did, if she did anything else at all. Where she got the flowers.

And then there was the day the old woman wasn't there, and she wasn't there the next day either, and Faye asked her mother but her mother didn't understand what Faye was try-ing to say. What woman? her mother said.

Now, as Faye drove into the neighborhood, she grew confused: the lanes folded one into another, appearing identical to each other. Or identical to the specific one she was searching for. They were all long and narrow with row houses and telephone lines and clothes drying in the air. But the market was there and she parked and browsed the stalls: the vendors selling herbs, jewelry, postcards of the Pudong skyline, masks for the smog. A man was crouched on the ground, weaving baskets. As she watched him she thought about what she would like to do in another life.

What did she do in this one? She watched her father die. She left. She worked in a motel. She picked apples. She lived in barns that had been converted into dorms. She lived for over a decade in a country where she was never sure of the language. She was robbed, beaten, had her shirts torn off, and six times she was pinned to the ground while she frantically searched for her knife.

Probably she stabbed someone in that dark once. She didn't know. She never saw. She ran. She never cried but she cried over lost buttons on her shirt. Her coat.

She walked down the lanes. The sky had yet to clear. Some rooftops were hidden. She kept searching the balconies. The shape of clothes suspended in the air, those sudden colors fighting against the smog. She found a café. She didn't know if it was the one but she stopped and looked up at the row house beside it, up to the third floor where there was a young man on the balcony. He was wearing a mask and a baseball cap.

Faye waved. He stood and went inside. Perhaps she scared him. She looked into the café, trying to remember some detail, some corner. Her father had lost the apartment and they had never returned, spending the rest of the years in the countryside.

The row-house door opened and the young man was there.

You're the caretaker? he asked.

She didn't answer. A child ran into the café. The brief smell of baking bread. Tea.

Why are your jeans wet? the man said.

I was by the sea, Faye said.

He considered this. He was her age. Perhaps a few years older. The baseball cap was blue and had an orange sign on it she didn't know.

Shanghai is sinking, he said. He pointed up at the smog. Warm weather, he said. Rising water. Water goes high. We sink.

You know things, Faye said.

I know nothing, he said. Come on. You're late.

He left the door open. She stepped inside. She followed him up the stairs to the third floor, past the landings and a hallway window. He was faster than she was. He was already in the apartment by the time she came up. He took her hand and brought her into a short corridor where there were slippers and coats on a rack. She kept her hand in his, hearing a television.

The kitchen would be on the left, she thought, and on the right would be the main room where there was the balcony. The last would be where they all slept.

They ended in the main room. The man was leading her to someone on the couch when Faye noticed a painting on the wall. She caught the colors of it, the slopes and the ridge, and she would never be certain if it was the one that had been theirs and someone else's before that but she froze, stilled by it. And as she began to cry she covered her mouth and looked away, waiting for it to pass.

The man brought her to the couch. A much older man was sitting on one end. He hadn't moved. She thought he had been watching the television but when she calmed she saw the gray blur in his eyes.

Cataracts, the young man said. I don't know what that is but he has it. That's my grandfather. He doesn't speak. You can take care of him now. Father will be home in four hours.

He raised four fingers. He hadn't taken off his mask or his baseball cap. Faye wiped her eyes. The grandfather lifted his hands and waited. She leaned forward and he pressed his hands against her face, studying her features.

He'll do that all day if you don't stop him, the man said. He's weird.

She didn't mind. She couldn't explain but it wasn't like being touched by hands. It felt like leaves.

She asked if the café below still sold flowers.

The man didn't know.

Lady, he said. You're weird.

I'm tired, Faye said. And I'm sick.

He sighed. He entered the bedroom. On the television there was a news report on the smog affecting cameras, so many of them crashing or getting lost. She looked out at the balcony, at the corner near the rail, imagining herself there as a child. The man came back out and waved her in.

He had attempted to make the bed inside. The blinds were drawn; she had trouble seeing into the room. She made out the mattress. A blanket and a mattress.

I'll do the first shift, he said. You rest. You get better.

He slipped off his mask and his baseball cap. He didn't look the way she had guessed. She rose from the couch and he sat down by his grandfather and switched the channel to a music video. He reached over the coffee table and picked up a cup with soda. She listened to the suck of the straw. The grandfather was watching her. Or it felt as though he was. The young man nodded and waved.

Go in, he said.

V.

In the days that followed she visited them. She spent whatever money she had on food she had never eaten herself in years and gave it to them and they ate together watching a movie on the television. She met the father, too. He was shy and ate faster than any of them. If the caretaker ever showed they never mentioned it. It was always just them. She sat in the middle with these three men on the couch or on the floor, spending an hour or two when she could.

Some nights she was too weak to go. Or too weak to head back, and they let her stay. When her nausea returned she slipped into the bathroom and did it quietly, with the door locked, the way she did in her room these days, with the new window blinds she had bought pulled down.

The pain seemed less. Or she had grown used to it and could manage it better. Or she was better able to brace herself for it. The bruise, however, never went away. It remained on her cheek, the size of a coin, though no one noticed. If they did they didn't say. At the factory it was covered by her mask. She wore it every day.

She kept assembling cameras. She was given a new post at another station, and she recognized a piece of the bracelet she was putting together. There were fewer people on this line. It was more quiet. She felt at ease here, she grew less tired. She had a different manager at this station. On occasion, she would see the other one, crossing the lot to his car, his arm wrapped around Yonha and whispering something into her ear. Sometimes Yonha looked back, and Faye thought she saw in her expression a sadness. Then Yonha would embrace him with all her strength and bury her face in his neck as they went away.

The woods along the river began to change. Faye saved enough money to buy a winter coat and boots at a used clothing store. She bought a teapot, too, and sometimes in the evening she would make tea and lean over the rail and look out at the river and the boats, the tire fortress in the playground. The falling leaves.

She didn't go out often other than to see the family in the lane house, though once she went to the skating rink on the outskirts of the city. She went with a few families and Yonha's daughter, who were all practicing for the winter and the frozen river. She had less of an appetite now but they shared a bucket of popcorn. Neon lights blinked in the rafters. She sat and watched everyone spin and turn, approach each other and move apart again.

Out of habit, she saved the Styrofoam cups from the skating rink vending machine. In her room she stacked them in different shapes along one wall, balancing as many as she could. It was something to do.

One night someone knocked on her door. She had come in from the showers. She had changed and was sitting on the floor, flipping through a magazine she had found in the trash container. It was a travel magazine, thick and heavy, and she had been flipping through the photos. Montreal. A vineyard in France. Siberia.

She opened the door to find Tad there, chewing on a fingernail, almost shy. It had been over two months. His face had healed. He looked the way she remembered him at the bus stop. But there were still bandages wrapped around his hand. He was carrying a bag over his shoulder and his sunglasses in his shirt pocket. He had just arrived.

She wanted him to smile. When he did she moved into him, slipping her arms around his waist. She listened to him breathe.

Is there gas in the tank? he said.

Yes.

He took her hand and they went down to the lot where she kept his scooter. Tad let her drive. He slipped in behind her and held her and she turned north up the river road, away from the city and the factories.

It grew into evening. They drove under a clear sky, speed-ing past a boat on the river. She was wearing her winter coat. She spotted the bend and the old wooden sign and slowed, turning onto the dirt road. They got out by the fence and Tad carried his bag with him. He kept his bandaged hand close to his chest. They followed the path through the mounds of gar-bage, down the slope to the roped-in ring where the lights were turning on.

No one had arrived yet. Only a few of the fighters who were warming up. Tad introduced Faye to the two he knew, the two he had brought over. They spoke briefly in Korean to each other and when Faye answered them their eyes bright-ened in surprise.

They were brothers. They were each fighting. Faye asked if they ever fought each other. They laughed. They were hop-ping on their feet, warming themselves. Only outside the ring, they said, and pretended to swing at each other.

She liked their playfulness. Their conviviality. The bond of family. It changed what she was about to see.

Tad had moved across the ring. He was kneeling over his bag, fumbling. She went over and knelt and before she un-derstood what he was doing he clipped a bracelet on her.

They want to record the fight, Tad said.

He pressed a button, releasing the camera and it hovered

in the air, whirring. The screen came up. He told her she could adjust the screen size. It could be as small as a mobile phone or as large as a window. There was a track pad on the bracelet against which she pressed her finger to navigate the camera. She tracked up and the camera followed her movement. She flicked her finger over the pad, fast, and the camera gained speed, heading into the sky.

She kept watching the screen. The speed of what she was seeing. The elevation. A cloud fragment. A leaf. The images shook and blurred. Tad adjusted the sensitivity of the track pad, to better match her movements. They practiced for an hour.

In that time a crowd had formed by the ring. A woman walked around with a tablet, recording bets. Faye walked back up the slope. She stayed at that distance, looking through the screen. She hovered over the audience, recognizing the men wearing tuxedos and smoking cigars.

Then the fight started and she began to record it, from above. She heard cheering. She kept the camera just over the string of lights and as the rounds went on she lowered the camera so that she could film at different angles. The image shook a bit but it settled and she captured footwork and the swings, the fighters' faces.

Tad checked in, climbing the slope, and they watched the

fighters on the screen together. Faye stood to stretch. She turned to find the moon and stopped. In the high mountain across the river, she caught a faint light. She turned to Tad but he was concentrating on the screen.

Faye waited. In between fights, when no one was looking, she moved the camera away and flew it over the woods, across the river. She pushed it higher. She watched as it skimmed the mountain slope, over the canopy, flying past the lights on the distant ridge. She slowed it down. She turned the camera around. She brought it lower and returned to where she had seen the lights.

It was a large house. A tiled roof. A garden. Behind her she heard a horn. Clapping. Then, on the screen, in the field behind the large house, a strange, pale tree.

The first brother won. The other lost. They remained in good spirits, collecting the money they made. They met girls. The girls took them in their cars into Shanghai. It was nearing dawn. She had come down from the slope and returned the camera to Tad. When the ring was clear he collapsed on the ground and stretched out.

Let me be, he said. Let me sleep.

She sat beside him and ran her hands through his hair.

I want you to come with me somewhere, she said.

He was drifting, looking up at the brightening sky.

Anywhere, he said. After I sleep.

She flicked a finger against his face, waking him.

What happened to your cheek? he said.

I fought, she said.

He didn't respond.

Tad, she said.

He hummed a song. He began to drift again.

Tad, she said. Please come.

He opened his eyes and yawned. He got up and held her face, looking at her. She helped him stand.

They took the scooter farther down the river, looking for a road that would lead them up into the mountain. She found it a kilometer away, steep, unpaved, and Tad doubted the scooter would be able to climb. She tried, driving up the slope as the road grew steeper and they began to wind around the side of the mountain. Here the leaves had all fallen. They drove over them and over sandbags that some-one had placed in a gap where flooding had destroyed the road one year. They drove for almost an hour, climbing.

She could feel hints of morning when she saw the house from a distance. It was in the old style with a gate and a courtyard. It was a mansion. They pulled into the driveway where she could see the remnants of the garden she had seen from above, a pond that had not been cleaned. The windows were dark and one of the main doors was ajar.

They parked in the front. She pulled out her father's pocketknife from her boot, and for the first time Tad looked at her, concerned. Puzzled. She took his hand and they entered, coming upon a hall of some kind. An abandoned hall with high rafters and holes in the ceiling so that there were towers of dim light everywhere, illuminating the broken pieces of statues that once stood against the walls. The statues of horses, their heads, their hooves, their armor. There was the sound of water dripping somewhere. She was holding Tad when she almost screamed, watching as one of the broken statues sighed and rose, stepped over the others, and approached them, shaking off dust. The two of them not yet understanding that it wasn't a ghost but an actual horse that slipped by them and down the hallway. The great echo of its hooves. As though, living on the mountain, it sought the company of its own image.

They followed it, passing a piano in the corner with its top gone, revealing the insides. Faded tapestries hung on the walls. At the end was a door that led outside. The horse stepped out onto a paddock and trotted away.

It was as though they had stumbled upon somewhere even farther than where they were. Her feet ached. Her body. She ignored the growing pain under her rib. She took off her shoes and left them in the corridor. She let go of Tad and crossed the field, heading toward the pale tree. She didn't know if he was behind her. She heard nothing. She kept walking until she was there. The disfigured branches. Her father who had climbed this mountain and walked here, already dying, too weak to go on any farther. What had he planned to do? He collapsed under the tree. The chemical plant owner had found him the next day, still breathing, the knife locked in her father's hand.

There was a stable in the distance. She caught the flash of a small flame in a stall. She gripped the knife. The other horses had sensed her and were peering out, their eyes catching what remained of starlight.

She saw his cigarette glow before she saw him. He had been brushing a horse. But it wasn't him, it wasn't whom she thought it would be, whom she wanted it to be. It was someone else, someone she didn't know. He wore tall rubber boots and had a gray beard. She had never seen a horse so close before. It distracted her. Its grandeur. Its ease and slowness, the earth smell of the coat and the slopes of the neck, the way the muscles curved.

Here, the man said.

He offered her the comb. Like this.

He had seen the knife. He waited. She didn't know what to do. She tucked the knife in her waistband and took the comb. He guided her hand, pressing the comb against the horse's flank and circling.

It loosens the dirt and dead hair. Massages the coat.

She hadn't yet spoken. He kept his hand over hers and they curried the horse. He let go. She kept currying.

Good, he said, and left the stall and went out into the paddock she had crossed. He sat on a bench and faced the field and the far tree. The abandoned mansion.

He didn't look back when he said, You are one of the children.

She stayed with the horse.

The ones who swam in the river, he said. You're the only ones who ever come up here.

She stopped. She felt the horse shift and turn its head toward her and nudge. Across the field, she saw Tad talking to an older woman. She wore a long wool coat like Faye's and her hair was braided. She was inspecting his bandaged hand.

Someone came up here? Faye said.

Sure. Someone always comes up. Someone like you. Looking for him. Looking for who knows what. For something to make them feel better.

She asked where they were, whether any of them were still alive but he didn't know.

And him? she asked. Where is he?

He shot himself. Years ago. Here.

He slapped the bench. He said that he had been the groundskeeper. He had taken care of the horses, too.

So no one is here?

I'm here, the groundskeeper said.

He pointed across the field at the woman who was now holding the camera.

My wife is here, he said.

As it grew lighter she could make out the smaller house near the mansion, where the two still lived.

She heard Tad's voice traveling toward them. He and the woman had wandered away from the tree. For a moment they were huddled together and then Tad stepped back and the woman lifted her arm as the camera detached itself from her wrist. It flew up slowly, then gained speed and disappeared into the sky.

Have you told him? the groundskeeper said.

Told him?

For the first time the groundskeeper turned around to look at her in the stable.

You clench your hands. You're often nauseous. You rub

the side of your stomach because there is something there and you don't want to get help for it because your father didn't and you're afraid.

She ignored him and went back to currying the horse. She shook her head.

Will you? he said.

Tell him? she said. I don't know.

Tell him, he said.

She left the horse and joined the groundskeeper on the bench. She was still holding the comb. She placed it on the bench beside her and then took out the knife, too. She laid it beside the comb and ran her toes through the grass.

What happened to the tree? Faye said.

From across the distance, morning came into the mountain.

MILNER FIELD

I.

Before my father died, he told me a story.

He was still well enough to walk, and I had taken him, along with my daughter, Philippa, to the park. It was where he liked to go every day since his retirement. For forty years my father had been a doctor in a town in New York, a few hours north of the city, and he ended up staying there, having grown accustomed to the climate and the region—the great river and valley, the apple cider and the dairy, the golf courses, the stories of Washington Irving and the novels of James Fenimore Cooper.

His favorite English word was: *foliage*. I remember he

used to practice saying it out loud in front of the mirror in his bedroom before he went to his office so that he could have something sociable to talk about with his patients. I would be sitting on the edge of the bed, wearing his lab coat, the pockets of which held parking receipts, chewing-gum wrappers, and his stethoscope, not wanting our neighbor, who was my sitter, to arrive. I would watch as he tied his necktie, spritzed on some kind of fragrance, and said into the mirror, *Foliage*, as though it were the gravest or most profound of matters. And sitting there behind him, staring at his reflection, I said it back to him, slipping on his stethoscope and listening to my heart and the strangeness of my own voice.

My father had emigrated from South Korea in 1976 and he used to tell me that he would go back one day, in particular in those early years after my mother passed, and I used to brace myself for this, for some kind of return for him and a leaving for myself.

I don't remember being disappointed or anxious or frightened by this possibility. I didn't have many friends, so it was always just us. And as long as there was this—us—I thought that I would manage. But I did, as a child, think of New York as a kind of temporary station, and a temporary life where I never wanted anything, or pretended to not want anything, hiding that desire for a new bicycle or a comic book for that elsewhere we would most certainly end up in.

Of course this never happened. We didn't go anywhere. I grew up. He grew old. And I did leave, to other places, but he stayed, picking up golf and taking walks in the park.

Maybe *park* isn't the word I am looking for. If I recall it was a nature preserve of some kind, with a parking lot and paths that wound their way through acres of land on the eastern side of the valley. There were long fields with wildflowers. An open structure the size of a barn that could be rented for performances and weddings. If you walked all the way to the end there were benches along a cliff overlooking the river, the bridge, and the city of Kingston on the other side of the valley. He liked sitting there and watching the cargo boats head upstate and to Canada. The freight train that appeared once a day in the afternoon. The hawks.

Sometimes he liked to tell me about the train he and his parents had hopped with fifty others to escape fighting during the war. His parents had convinced him that they were embarking on a great adventure. For a long time during that ride he didn't understand that something was wrong. That the country was on fire. He peered through the slats and for the first hour saw nothing, and then he saw everything. For three days he saw and heard everything from a train car the size of four beds.

I knew my father as someone who was reserved and shy, who was dedicated to his work and to his patients but who remained in the car when he picked me up from school, a parent who always cooked me dinner but left me alone in the kitchen to eat it. Someone who was both there and not there.

But once in a while he would tell me a story. A story from his life. It would come unexpectedly, as though he were finishing a private thought, and I liked listening, even if it was one he had already told me because we didn't speak very much throughout our lives, and when I was young a story felt like the two of us speaking, like he wanted me to be a part of whatever memory he had tunneled into.

The story he shared that day as we sat on a bench facing the valley was one I had never heard. Even now I am unsure why he spoke of it in that moment at all. I remember that he was very tired from the walk, and I felt guilty for urging him to go on so that we could reach the cliff. It was selfish of me, I knew, because my daughter, Philippa, was with us, and I wanted to impress her. She was six then. Seven years earlier I had met her mother, married her, and we had lasted until a few months ago. I still called her my wife. She had moved back to Berlin, and tomorrow Philippa would go back to her. I wasn't yet used to not seeing my daughter every day. Watching Philippa, in the high grass of the cliff, I was already missing her. And missing my wife.

She was German and a geologist, and one Christmas I was invited to a staff party at a restaurant, because I ate at the bar every Friday, to treat myself, so they called me a regular. I work with satellites, and the restaurant was near the office, so I would go there to watch the news or a part of a movie they were playing, and then return to the computers and the data.

There was a winter storm that Christmas and we all stayed the night. She was a friend of one of the waiters, and as the staff got more drunk she tended bar. I kept her company. She invented cocktails for me to sip. I made up names for them—the Mars Rover, the Panorama. I channel-surfed and found the burning Yule log. The storm grew worse, the snow growing heavy on the sidewalks. We made bets on whether she was in fact leaving for Delphi in two days. She was studying the Pythia. I didn't know what that was.

An oracle, she said. The Temple of Apollo. The oracle would stand there on Parnassus and inhale vapors that came up from fissures in the mountain and it would induce something like a seizure and she would speak nonsense, which the priests interpreted as prophecies.

I wondered what this had to do with geology. She was beautiful there in the bar light and the reflections on the glasses, the fire on the television.

No, the vapors, she said. I'm studying the vapors. The rocks.

Outside the snow kept falling. Through the windows we watched people race into the empty street and wrestle. She leaned over the bar. I didn't yet know her name. She took my cell phone and input her number and the name, the Pythia. It's still there.

Here is what my father told me that day on the cliff:

When my father was young he had a Japanese friend, a neighbor, someone he saw every day, during school and after. He was younger than my father and his name was Takashi Inoue. This was in the 1960s, long after the wars, and Takashi's father, who was Japanese and a professor, had been hired by a nearby university. Takashi's mother was Korean and a math tutor. Three days a week, after school, my father went there for extra lessons.

One day Takashi, who was eleven, went into his father's office and found a rifle hidden behind a box of clothes, letters, and photographs. The rifle was from a campaign in the Russian Far East and had been a gift from his father's commanding officer whose life he had saved. The officer had fallen down a cliff and Takashi's father had gone in search of him, eventually finding him on the bank of a river with a broken leg. In the chaos of a retreat, they survived a journey back through the valley.

The rifle, though, wasn't the officer's. He had found it on their way back, lying not far from the Russian it had once belonged to, the only hint of who the soldier was in another life in a folded sheet of music tucked inside his chest pocket. The officer took it and, years later, it lay in a wooden case, one that Takashi thought contained something else, for he knew his father not as a war veteran but as a geography teacher, and someone who had started a new hobby: taking photos. It was his father's camera Takashi was looking for that day, fascinated by the intricacies of photography.

He found the rifle instead. He picked it up, unsure of how even to hold the thing. He aimed, or imagined how one aimed. He pointed it toward the window. Then, hearing footsteps—his sister's footsteps or his mother's—he put the rifle away and returned it to where it was.

Takashi didn't tell anyone what he did. Not his sister, who was older, or his mother, and certainly not his father, whom he adored but about whose life he had just discovered some new passage to explore.

A few days went by. The week. Takashi did his homework. He went to school. After, my father visited. As I said, he was older, and perhaps Takashi was in awe of him or wanted to impress him, so he took my father's hand. They went down the hall and snuck into the office. I don't know where Takashi's sister was then. I know their mother was at the opposite end of the house, where she tutored students.

It was a single-story house, and long, and my father remembered how the shiny floors caught their reflections as they ran across them all the time, infuriating the nanny. Drawings and old photos of Russia hung on the walls. There was a library. And there was always a spare set of slippers left out for when he visited. It was a good life they had, the Japanese family. It was a privileged one. They weren't unaware of this. They weren't unaware that my father's father—my grandfather—was not a teacher but worked in the shop where the family's housekeeper came to purchase milk, comic books, and cigarettes.

My father could not remember why they brought the rifle out to the hallway. Perhaps they were in an imagined world where a certain distance was necessary. More fun. Perhaps it was a way to acknowledge that it was now a shared discovery, no longer a secret but something they could call their own. Perhaps they just wanted to show off for Takashi's sister. He couldn't remember either, whether they called to her or whether she had heard them and appeared at the opposite end of the hall. She approached. They could hear a student repeating out loud an equation. A piano on the radio.

Look! Takashi said, and pointed, and Takashi's sister did, when she was closer. And when she saw what her brother was holding, she stopped.

Come look, Takashi said, shaking the rifle, and that was when the rifle went off.

The rifle went off and there was a spark and the noise entered my father and passed as suddenly as he heard it. And his body jerked, feeling something like a hand hit his chest and move through him. He shut his eyes, knowing something was wrong. He wanted to fall but when he opened his eyes he saw it wasn't him but Takashi's sister in the air and falling. And then everything was silent. And for what seemed like a long time my father did nothing. And Takashi, not understanding what had just occurred, still holding the weapon, did nothing. And the nanny came. And their mother came. And the student who had been solving equations came. And Takashi's sister, on the wooden floor, shook. She shook and she went still. She went still looking up, or what she must have thought of as up, for she was on her side. She was looking, when she died, through the open doorway of a bedroom. The window held a clear fall day. A thin shadow. Light on the floor.

She was fifteen years old. My father's age. On the same day, in an act of desperation or madness or both, Takashi was sent away, never to see that house or that town or his family again.

Takashi never saw my father again either. And my father never knew where it was he had been sent. But he used to always believe that Takashi would one day come back. That his parents would bring him back. He used to wait and wonder if that was the plan, if there was a plan in the recklessness of their minds.

But they never did. Bring him back. And Takashi's parents attempted to continue their lives for a few more years after that but then left as well, for somewhere else, moving into a small apartment where they spent the rest of their life, my father said, vanishing into themselves.

As I said, I don't know why he told me all this that day. Or why he never told me until that day. He told me and then he didn't say anything else. The freight train appeared and he watched it move north beside the river. He finished his bottled water. I could read nothing in his expression. It was a fine fall afternoon. I was leaving the next morning.

A young couple came to enjoy the view. They had a beautiful dog that bounded forward and licked Philippa on the knee. This frightened her, and she screamed. The man and the woman rushed to us but I assured them it was all right. It's all right, I said, to them and to my daughter, and I took her on my lap but she had already gotten over it and was staring at the dog, staring as it sulked through the high grass as though embarrassed or ashamed. Perhaps Philippa sensed this. I felt her take my wrists in a way that surprised me in its adult confidence and she slipped off my legs and followed the dog.

My father, who had been silent through all this, greeted the couple, and commented on the beautiful dog and then the foliage. And as I watched Philippa try again with the dog, as the sound of the train faded, my father took my shoulder and stood.

I wasn't used to his touch. I felt his weight leaning on me for a moment before he switched to his cane. Across the meadow, Philippa reached out her hand. The dog nosed her fingers. They were on the cliff's edge. A strong wind came, blowing my daughter's hair, and suddenly my father rushed to her, picked her up with one arm, and returned. It happened so quickly, he had moved so quickly, I was still on the bench as he returned Philippa, who was smiling, to me.

Let's go home, my father said.

That was the last day I saw my father alive. The next morning I said good-bye to him and drove to the airport, where I escorted Philippa through security and got her a pink lanyard with a card that read: *Unaccompanied Minor.*

There were dog hairs stuck to her jacket. I picked them off and showed them to her. She was delighted that the hair was the same color as hers, a pale blond Philippa inherited from her mother. She opened her pencil case and put them there. I caught the smell of shampoo or soap on her skin as she hugged me, told me to visit soon, and boarded the plane. I sat by the gate window. I left a message on my father's phone and then my hands shook and I didn't know what to do, so I stayed, long after the plane taxied away, looking down at the patterns of the terminal carpet, understanding somehow that my world had altered but not yet knowing how.

I am an only child. Though I didn't keep the house, I kept his old stethoscope, which, I was surprised to read, in his messy handwriting, was willed to me.

II.

For a time after my father died, I thought he shared the story of Takashi Inoue because it was a regret, a regret that they were never able to see each other again. But I eventually convinced myself that the reason he told me was in fact a request: my father wanted me to find his childhood friend.

I tried for a year. I contacted other family members of mine. My father's sisters, who had scattered all over, from Germany to Los Angeles. I searched online. I wrote letters to agencies and orphanages in South Korea, Japan, Russia, and China. I thought Takashi must have gone back to Japan or had gone to Russia or China.

I had dreams about him. In the dreams I was the age I was but he was always a young boy. And the locations were always different. Sometimes we met on a bridge. Other times on the train, the two of us opening a window at night and poking our heads out into the evening and the bright moon. His face was so clear, as though we had known each other since I myself was a child, a face that always vanished from my mind when I woke.

Of course nothing came up. It was impossible to fathom how many people were displaced and moving and migrating during those many years after the Korean War. How long that went on for. There were some people with the same name, who would have been around the same age, who kindly wrote back, apologizing. There were children who wrote back. I received a copy of the death certificate of one who had been a sailor and had drowned when his ship sunk. I received another of a thief who had been murdered; yet another, an engineer, who died peacefully, in old age.

He was none of them. Or he could have been any of them.

In many ways, I knew how silly this was. I was often embarrassed, sending yet another letter, receiving yet another one back. Of course there were times when I didn't know why I was doing this, when I didn't want to look for him anymore. I woke one day and realized a year had passed. My life unchanged. My wife, who was no longer my wife, still in Berlin, or wherever she was traveling to for her sites. My daughter still splitting her time between me and her.

So I stopped. I gave up. We all grew older, Philippa suddenly into an adult, taller than me, healthier. There was a period in her life when she liked to take photographs, and once, she sent me prints of her house in Berlin—the front door, the light in the hallway, the speck of her mother in a room—and I thought of him and was tempted to try again. But I didn't, I knew it would be the same, that I would find nothing. On occasion, over the years, he reappeared in my dreams but in the dream I hurried past him, pretending I didn't know him until I woke.

I wonder whether I would have ever returned to it.

Whether I would have continued the search at another point in my life. Philippa was studying abroad in London one year. She was crossing an intersection and forgot to look right instead of left. The car pummeled into her, and the wheel caught her leg, carrying it up into the undercarriage and dragging her toward the lamppost half a block away.

Philippa was twenty-two. She survived but her leg from the knee down was amputated almost immediately and she spent three months in physical therapy in London. Her mother and I took turns staying with her. During those months I worked in the London office. I slept on the company couch or at the hospital. I used to wake and find her scratching some empty space on her bed, in her half sleep believing the rest of her leg was still there. Other times she would wake shouting, begging for the itch to go away.

It was the same summer as the Underground bombings and the bus explosion in Tavistock Square. We watched it from a television in Philippa's room. I turned the television off but Philippa took the remote from me and kept watching in silence, her eyes unblinking as my phone began to ring.

In the London office they had Tavistock Square up on the screen, a few minutes after it occurred. The mangled bus, the smoke. Someone I worked with, a young man, hit the rewind button. Then the footage played and we saw a figure being propelled backward into the iron fence of the park.

That month I requested a transfer and moved to England. Philippa was still in physical therapy and I spent every day with her. I brought the curry she liked. I watched her try on her prosthetic. I watched her walk and swim. We played board games and thumb-wrestled. She liked the pool, the cool water, the strokes. I would sit on a bench as she swam and call her mother. Sometimes she answered. I don't remember anymore if we talked about anything other than Philippa, whether I had called for something else. I saw the arc of our daughter's arm over the water and there was the comfort of a voice I had known in another life.

At the end of fall, Philippa was moved to a rehab center in Berlin, to be with her mother. During that time I kept watching the satellite data of Tavistock Square. I had copied the file and brought it home with me. Maybe the office knew. They never said. I stayed awake at nights and from my laptop I watched two people on the bench in the square, in the moment before the bus approached. I had missed them the first time. Perhaps they were on a date or eating or reading a book. There was something on the bench between them but I could never tell what it was. A bag or a hat. Flowers. I watched them there and then they were gone.

*   *   *

I lived in those years in a flat in Southwark, off of Bermondsey Street. It was on the second floor of a converted warehouse. It was owned by the company I worked for. When
Philippa recovered she often visited me, taking one of the
budget airlines across the continent, and I picked her up at
Gatwick.

Philippa liked the place because you had to enter through
the store on the ground floor and take the cargo elevator.
It was a furniture store then, selling bed frames and coffee
tables made of reclaimed wood and salvaged metal. I got
along with the workers there, seeing them often as I passed
through the floor, and they kept trying to set me up with
someone. They were young and filled with a kind of yearning
that I once saw in my wife in our first year together, when
she would lead me somewhere away from everyone else so
that we could continue the privacy we had begun to create
and cherish in our marriage.

Some nights when the store was empty Philippa and I
would sneak down and try the furniture. We would lie on a
bed or a couch and she would, in a mock art-gallery tone, explain to me the trendiness of the piece we had claimed. I had
brought down my laptop and popcorn and as we watched a
movie, I tried my best not to ask about her mother, who had

remarried by then, to one of her colleagues. They seemed to live a glamorous life, in their world traveling.

I don't know why it didn't work between my wife and me. She was often away. I got used to her being away and without being aware of this at first, I began to form a life that no longer included her. She took up less and less space in my mind. I understood it was the same for her. That it would always be this way.

I told Philippa this one evening, in the furniture store, when she was in her thirties. I think we were binge-watching a sitcom in the dark. I had begun to study the furnishings of the apartment the comedy was always set in, wondering how many times it changed. What new decorations and kitchenware they came up with.

Outside the warehouse, a man walked by on the cobblestone street and peered in. He was carrying a bottle of wine and was drinking from it. He stepped back, his body in silhouette, and he swayed. He hadn't seen us. Only the faint glow of the laptop screen. Philippa rested her head on my shoulder. It was summer. She had come from France, after a monthlong excavation in the Pyrenees. Philippa, child of a geologist and a satellite programmer, had become an archaeologist.

The site was on El Camino de Santiago. They were help-

ing the UN uncover the bodies of victims who perished trying to reach Spain during the Second World War. She didn't
feel like saying more that day. She was tired but happy to be
with me. I had given her a watch as a gift before she left, and
she was wearing it that night while the show played at a low
volume, the screen light flashing blue across her face.

Saint James's Way, Philippa said. The translation of El
Camino de Santiago. Or Way of Saint James. I wonder if
there's a difference depending on how you say it.

Philippa liked language—translations, etymology. She
had been studying linguistics in London that year.

Saint James, I said.

Patron saint of Spain, she said, and unbuckled her prosthetic.

On the show a woman slumped on the couch and began
to cry. I had missed the cause. There was a pause and then
someone opened the apartment door wearing a *Mask of Zorro*
costume, with a sword even, and the laugh track roared. I
didn't know why but we laughed along with it. And then the
episode ended and the screen went dark. In the momentary
silence we could hear the heavy footsteps of the drunk man
outside continuing down toward the river.

You broke each other's hearts, Philippa said, still leaning
on my shoulder.

I rested my head against hers and squeezed her hand.

Yes, I said.

I thought she would say more, but she didn't. I thought she was angry with me. Or sad. I tried to recall the last time we had held hands. I looked down and saw that Philippa had fallen asleep and was breathing heavily, almost a snore. I laughed. She didn't wake. I flicked popcorn off her shirt. I unclasped the watch, adjusted the strap size, and put it on her again.

I didn't see her for a long time after that. Like her mother, she was on other trips, other sites, other digs. I worried about her leg. When we spoke on the phone, she sounded happy and full of energy, ambitious and stubborn, determined to work as much as she could.

During Christmas one year she surprised me by appearing in London with a duffel bag. We ate out every night and celebrated the New Year with the furniture store workers at a bar on Bermondsey Street. From across the room I saw her wrap her arms around one of the men and kiss him. I smiled, looked away. She got drunk. She got drunk enough to tell them what we did, what we had been doing for years in their store, and the workers shouted and dragged us back and we all sat on the furniture and listened to music on my laptop. I watched as my daughter leapt down from a mattress and

grabbed the cane she sometimes used to play some air gui-
tar. Her long hair glowing in the dark. There were shadows
around her, dancing.

Every year from then on she came, always in the fall or
the winter, and through the years we began to explore England together, heading south into Wales and east to Suffolk
and then north, until that year when we reached the very tip
of Scotland. She was in her forties by then. I remembered
my father on a bench on a cliff. We had reached another one
here. And this time the sea.

III.

There was a long period of time when I forgot about Takashi
Inoue. Then one day I met someone who reminded me of all
this again.

I had arrived early in North Yorkshire for a vacation with
Philippa. This was years before we had reached Scotland. She
had booked us two rooms in what had been an estate of some
kind. Philippa wasn't coming until two days later, though,
so I had some time alone. I was skeptical about the place,
worried it was too much of a tourist trap but Philippa had
promised that it would be wonderful.

The estate was called Milner Field. I read about the place. You could ride horses, go on hikes, get lost in the maze of a garden, shoot clay pigeons. The grounds, of course, were haunted. There had been a mill here, before the mansion was built. The husband had been a mill worker and had died in an accident at the factory. The story was that the wife he left behind continued to roam the property.

Haunted! Philippa said over the phone, and for a moment she sounded like she did when she was very young.

Milner, Philippa said. Perhaps from *miller*.

The silo collapsed and the husband was crushed under the weight of the grain.

The entire property, including the main house, a mansion—with its original Gothic architecture—had been converted into a hotel. As I arrived I could make out the brick turrets and the peaked rooftops, a paddock field with horses, a tall fountain. Waiting by the entrance, there were men dressed in old uniforms. One of the men opened the door to my taxi, asked the driver to please open the trunk, and the driver looked back at me. I was embarrassed to admit that someone had taken my luggage by accident on the train up, thinking it was their own. I had been told it was en route on the train the day after.

This was the first time a luggage complication had happened to me. I liked packing light and most times I had only a bag under my seat. But Philippa wanted to dress up one night for a fancy dinner at the mansion, so I had packed formal wear, which was also in the luggage.

Perfectly understandable, sir, he said, and I was touched by the sincerity in his voice.

He promised they would deliver the bag tomorrow to the room. He was in his twenties and polite and quick on his feet and escorted me inside where I was left, for a moment, breathless.

It was true: it was wonderful. I had never seen such a chandelier before. It was both elegant and reckless, as though the sun had been captured about to burst. There was red carpet on the marble. Statues of horses. Oil paintings in gilded frames. I smelled perfume in the air, mild and pleasant, and I wished my father were here. He would have been speechless. I would have made an awkward joke to get him to laugh.

I was checked in, and they confirmed the arrival of my daughter in two days. The woman behind the desk was also young, much younger than Philippa, and as she handed me the key she wished me a happy birthday.

If she caught the confusion on my face she didn't show it. I understood a moment later that Philippa had lied, as she did on occasion, to see if the hotel would do anything special for guests who were celebrating their birthdays or their anniversaries.

They did. We had our connecting rooms on the fourth floor and in mine they had set up a plate of chocolates on the table by the window. *Happy Birthday!* was written on the plate in ganache. They had also brought up a bottle of wine. I drank the wine that night, trying to get used to the old style of the room with its velvet drapes and antique furniture. My phone rang. It was the office, and I ignored it. I had trouble sleeping. I wasn't tired. Perhaps I was anxious for Philippa to get here. Perhaps I felt a bit out of place.

I wandered the halls for a while, looking at the tapestries and the paintings. I couldn't hear anyone else. My footsteps echoed. I stepped more loudly and then softly and did it again, listening. I passed still lifes and more velvet curtains, running my hands over them. Through a hall window there was a view of the shooting area. It was a clear night and as I gazed out at the property I realized I was waiting for the ghost to appear. I sat on the bench for a while.

I didn't see the mill worker's wife but I did see a horse. It must have gotten loose. It was a bay, I think, I couldn't tell in the dark. I tracked it grazing and then, to my surprise, it looked up. It looked up, I thought, in my direction, and then it went on, away from the stable, farther into the field.

*   *   *

I did manage to sleep but only a few hours that night. The next day I woke early and went for a walk outside, had breakfast at the bar, and began reading a novel Philippa had sent to me. There was a light rain. The sound of it on the glass was pleasant and calming, and it began to match the rhythm of the background music. Or perhaps I was imagining this as I read the first chapter of the novel.

For years she sent me copies of books she had read. Never new copies but hers. Every now and then I noticed her handwriting or a sentence she outlined, and even sometimes there was a small note for me on the margins, saying hello, wondering if I was in fact reading the book, promising she would test me later. I don't know why but I always wrote back to her on those margins, answering, Yes, or asking a question about the plot.

The restaurant and the bar were almost empty. An older couple sat in the far corner of the restaurant, not looking at each other. The television was on. The news. I grew restless. I wasn't sure what to do. I had the day to myself. I had two voice mails. The first was from work again and the second was from Philippa, saying she was excited to see me tomorrow, wondering how I was settling in. I tried calling her back but she didn't answer. I wished I had cleaner clothes. I had never been to this region before. I lingered by the bar, flipping through the hotel guide and the brochures of the moors and the rivers. Several movies had been filmed in this area.

I heard airplanes fly by low, low enough so that when I turned I could see the RAF logo on the tails. The bartender told me there was an air base nearby. It drove the horses mad. I thought he was the man who had greeted me when I first arrived but it wasn't. It was his brother, and they were twins, and he grinned and said I wasn't the first person to make that mistake.

I wondered how they were both here, working at the hotel together. He said they grew up in the town. It was what they did over the summer. Work at Milner Field. Staff, grounds keeping, food service.

I asked what town that was, the one he grew up in.

Thoralby, he said. Just down the road.

He collected my plate, wiped the counter, and refilled my water. There was a game on with Newcastle United and we watched it together for a bit.

In the early afternoon I checked with reception to see if my bag had come. She apologized, said it hadn't, and assured me that it would by the end of the day. She also offered me a gift certificate and pointed across the grand lobby to a store I hadn't seen when I arrived. Sundries. Chocolates, postcards, and bathing suits.

She was trying to be kind. The other brother, the one who stood attention at the entrance, walked in, waved to me, and asked how I was. Before I could respond he assured me my luggage would come.

I was going to say that I met his brother but I noticed the umbrella he was carrying, still wet, and asked if I could borrow it. Then I asked if they could point me in the direction of Thoralby.

The brother seemed puzzled. He looked at me as though uncertain why I would bother, and then concerned as though someone led me astray.

I wonder if there's a store there, I said. For clothes.

Oh, yes, he said. Certainly. Of course.

He said there was. The reception clerk offered to call me a taxi because of the rain but I felt like walking. The brother gave me his umbrella, a hotel umbrella, and told me to take a right at the end of the estate driveway.

So I walked that afternoon, in the countryside. It was a narrow lane and sometimes a car slowed so as not to splash me, and I was surprised by the courtesy of this. Drivers waved. I waved back. For a time two horses decided to follow me, along the fence, and I realized they must have thought I had a carrot or an apple for them. I wondered if one of them was the one I saw the night before. They followed until they couldn't, reaching the border of the property, and I left them as the lane sloped up and over a hill and a low stone wall appeared.

The rain never got heavy but it was consistent and soon my sneakers were soaked. My feet were cold. I was cold. Still I kept going. I was cold but happy. The landscape had made me happy. The long fields. The distant high hills covered in heather. I thought I would like to take Philippa on this walk and we could jump a fence and take one of the trails when it wasn't wet. We could go to the moors. Perhaps we could find an old English cottage for me to fix up and live in.

I walked for an hour. At an intersection, I followed the sign for Thoralby and descended into a village in the hills that was no longer than a few blocks of gray stone houses and a church. At the start of the street there was a rotary with a wide building that contained several stores, each of them with a fluorescent sign. I went toward the one that seemed like a clothing store, tried the door, not noticing the sign that stated that whoever worked there was out for lunch. I looked in. I saw camping equipment. Wellingtons. A wall of rifles.

I stepped back and took in the village. Smoke was rising

from chimneys. There was a pub across from the church. I thought I would go there, and I almost did, except I heard a bell ring farther down, a door opened, and a postman walked to his truck.

In that store window a toy train was circling the track, and a string of lights hung above it. Other things were on display, too. Pewter candlesticks. The torso of a mannequin wearing a Shetland sweater. It was a general store of some kind. I walked in and there were aisles of canned food, clothes, and miscellaneous gifts. More sundries. I smelled soup. In the corner, near the window, was a computer on a small desk, where a man in a wool shirt was checking his e-mail. A handwritten sign above listed the price per minute of logging on to the Internet.

I followed the aisles, found packages of underwear and T-shirts, socks, and picked up a sweater, too. I wondered if they had Wellies here. They did. I picked up a pair of those and then picked up another pair, guessing Philippa's size.

I didn't know how much any of this was. I didn't know why I kept picking things up and placing them on the counter. There was no one there. I was never so flagrant with expenses. I was still happy. My feet were cold and wet but I had enjoyed the walk and I was looking forward to seeing Philippa in a day.

I rang the counter bell. From behind a beaded curtain I saw a young woman come out, holding a bowl of soup, slurping noodles with a pair of chopsticks. She was, I thought, a Japanese woman. I wasn't sure if my face registered the surprise. She kept slurping noodles and seemed curious and indifferent at once. She had long, braided hair, wore very dark eyeliner, and her nose was pierced.

On holiday? she said.

She had a British accent.

Yes, on holiday, I said.

Where are you from?

In my life I have been asked this question enough to know in that moment that the woman wasn't asking where I lived.

Korea, I said. My parents were from Korea.

She placed her soup bowl next to my sweater and wiped her mouth with her hand. She grinned. She said a few phrases in Korean. I didn't hear it often in my life these days. I raced to open that old corner of my memory. I asked if she was Korean.

No, she said. My grandfather. He was born there. He used to live there. When he was young. His family did. You know. The great colony. Then he came here. I think. Or he went somewhere else first and then he ended up here. Anyway, he used to speak to me in Korean and I remember some phrases. Hello. How are you. Basic stuff.

I wondered why her grandfather had left Korea.

He was orphaned, the woman said. Lost his parents. He went to live with relatives. Sorry. I should know more about this. I didn't see him that much. He was always vague about it.

She shrugged. And then she grew embarrassed and looked down, suddenly aware that she was talking to a stranger.

I wanted her to go on. I was gripping one of the packages of socks.

I asked if her grandfather ended up here in Thoralby. She laughed.

No, she said. I did. I married a damn pilot. His family. It's their store.

A moment later we heard the engine of a jet pass over. She lifted a chain around her neck and kissed the cross there.

Superstition, she said. Habit. Just in case.

I said I understood.

He courted me from the air. You know that? He flew right down near the river in Norwich where I was in school and he was nearly expelled from the RAF because of that stupid stunt. He was so damn handsome.

It wasn't beyond me that she had just used the past tense.

You don't see him much, I said.

She shrugged and picked up her soup again.

It's nice to say something in Korean, she said. I didn't realize.

Yes, I said, and meant it. I didn't realize either. I hadn't spoken it very much since my father died.

The bell rang. We watched the man checking his e-mail leave. It snapped her out of wherever she was because she looked down at the clothes I had carried over from the aisles.

Staying awhile, are we?

I explained the luggage situation.

She rang it all up. It was twice as much as I guessed but I gave her my credit card and I heard the machine dial up and connect to the system. While we waited she packed every-thing with great care in a large paper bag, and even wrapped the sweater in tissue paper for me. She was about to hand the bag over when she asked me how I was returning to the hotel.

I'll walk, I said.

She looked outside. It was still raining. She looked at my umbrella and the bag.

Come on, she said, and went around the counter and I saw then that she was shorter than I was, she must have been standing on a platform of some kind. She put on a waxed cotton coat. Her own Wellingtons. I heard the rattle of keys in her coat pocket. She carried the bag out, and I followed her across the rotary to the small parking area, where she approached a scooter. She wiped down the seat. She gave me the bag, got on, and started the engine.

I'm Maya, she said. Put this on.

Maya handed me her spare helmet. Across the rotary two women were watching us. They were sitting in front of the church door, drinking tea.

They bought the church, Maya said. They'll renovate it and live there together. Gives the town something else to talk about. Usually they talk about me.

I suppose they'll talk about this, I said, and sat behind her.

Doubtful, she said, lit a cigarette, and pulled out of the rotary.

I had tucked the bag and the umbrella under one arm and the other I wrapped around her stomach.

Shy one, she said, blowing smoke into me, and I laughed and leaned in.

She went faster. We headed up the valley, turned, and soon we were driving back on the lane. We passed the stiles and distant sheep on the hills. The stone wall. The horses. The roof of the mansion appeared as we dipped down and up. The jet passed us, loud, and I saw Maya blow it a kiss and give it the finger. Then I leaned into her again and I stayed like that for the rest of the way.

Maya dropped me off in the afternoon. I stood with the brother at the entrance as she waved and went back down the driveway.

I see you met Maya, the brother said, and grinned.

I waited for him to go on but he went inside to help another guest.

I hadn't asked about her grandfather's name. I never would. I would see her a few more times but I didn't know this yet. Standing there, in front of the mansion, I was aware of the improbability of all this and yet I wondered why I wanted to believe that it was possible, that I had found a lost thread in my father's life.

I thought Maya would turn right, back into Thoralby, but she turned and sped the other way. Some horses followed her.

IV.

Philippa arrived later that afternoon. She surprised me by coming a day early. She came with her bags and mine as well. She had seen the taxi driver pick it up from the train station and recognized the tag on it. I shared a ride with your luggage, she said, and hugged me quickly, and said that I looked like shit.

She was wearing a large felt hat with a wide brim that covered her eyes. She told me it belonged to the person beside her, who forgot it on the plane, and she couldn't find the woman, had lost her in the disembarking crowd, and didn't know what to do.

So I kept it, she said, and tilted her head up so that I could see her eyes. What do you think?

She was glowing and awake and beautiful. My daughter Philippa. How much I loved saying this out loud to myself as though it were my secret, as though I were the only father in the world with a daughter.

The brother who was out front seemed enamored with her. I caught him looking her up and down and I jabbed him in the stomach, which confused her and made the brother's pale cheeks flush. He hurried to carry her bags in and she massaged her thigh. I asked her how she was.

Better now, she said, and slipped her arm under mine and we walked in.

The rain stopped. Philippa showered, changed, and knocked on the door connecting our rooms and threw two brochures at me.

This place is fabulous! she said, and wrapped her neck in the collar of the plush bathrobe she was wearing. I'm never leaving.

She wasn't wearing her prosthetic. As she threw herself on my bed, I wondered how often she thought of that day. I had saved her some chocolate, and she ate them all, one by one. I opened the brochures. One was for horseback riding on the trails. The other was for clay pigeon shooting. They listed the times they were open. They were both beginning in ten minutes.

Choose one, she said.

Horses, I said.

Probably not a good idea, she said, and tapped her hip.

She rolled over the bed, reached down, and grabbed the shooting brochure from me.

Let's go fire some guns, she said, in a voice that was deep and with a drawl.

She slipped on her prosthetic. She tore open the socks I had bought, and took the sweater, too, liking the color. I gave her the Wellingtons. She asked where I got all this and I said the town down the road. She thought we could go tomorrow, and I agreed. I hadn't told her about Maya yet.

We rushed down and outside. Philippa was wearing her hat again. We found the path to the field that I saw on my first night here. The older couple from the restaurant were there, and an instructor was loading a trap. We spent some time introducing ourselves and then the instructor taught us how to hold and fire the shotgun and before I was able to comprehend it all we were given safety equipment and the game had begun.

The clay pigeons were released automatically, and we took turns shooting, attempting five targets each. The couple had done this before; they hit several. I missed. I was stunned and sore from the recoil. I watched Philippa take the gun, lift, aim, and fire. I heard the trap release another. I watched her do it again. And again. It was loud, even with our ears covered, and I felt it deep in my chest. I could smell the gunpowder. I could see it rise like a thin fog as we all took turns and kept shooting. Birds, terrified, flew away. We ignored them and kept going. I cheered on the older couple. Philippa hit one target in the air and she hollered and jumped, looking over at me.

And then, as quickly as it had begun, the hour was over. We said good-bye to the instructor. We promised to see the couple at the fancy dinner that evening. Our ears ringing, unused to the sudden quiet, Philippa and I wandered the grounds of the estate. We found fallen apples under a tree and pocketed them to feed the horses. We took a path that led down a long hill. I asked how her mother was. I asked how work was. I thought again about telling her what happened today but decided I would wait. She pointed at the sky, tracing the path of a light.

One of yours? she said.

She never asked me about what I did. She used to, when she was younger, but now she didn't.

I shrugged. I didn't care.

I don't care, I said, and gave the satellite the finger, and Philippa laughed out loud, her voice lingering in the trees.

We weren't paying attention to the time. As we turned back the sun began to fall behind the woods. The sky had cleared and some stars had come out. We climbed the hill. I caught Philippa rubbing her thigh. She had left her cane in her room.

We returned to the field where we had shot the clay pigeons. I suggested we rest for a moment and Philippa didn't argue. She leaned against the wood railing. The traps had been put away in the shed but all the pieces of the clay pigeons still lay scattered in the grass. There were pieces everywhere. Broken pieces and whole pieces, untouched, the size of plates. I saw nothing else in the field but that debris and I couldn't say why or what it was but in that moment, in the low light, with Philippa beside me, I grew afraid.

I wondered what she was thinking. I was thinking of her. I was thinking of her holding a gun and shooting and jumping and I was thinking of the screens at work and everything I had seen in the last fifteen years and had the technology to see. I thought of Maya and Takashi Inoue and the two people on the bench at Tavistock Square who were obliterated. I thought of a winter storm and a drink called the Mars Rover and the bridge and my father. I thought about the day when we wouldn't go on these trips anymore, and I wondered if Philippa would still go, alone, or with her mother, with someone else. If her life would be all that different when I was gone.

The sun went down. A wind came into the field and moved over us. Then the shadow of something small and quick flickered in the air, crossing our line of sight, briefly.

Maybe it's not from *mill*, Philippa said.

I didn't know what she was talking about.

Milner, she said. Maybe it's from Millinery. Milliner. Maker of hats.

Philippa tapped the one she was wearing. She took it off. I saw her eyes. Her bright eyes catching the early moon as she tossed the hat into the field. It spun, flipped, and landed in the grass.

I think her head must be cold, she said.

Who?

The ghost's, Philippa said, and then we made our way back to the hotel, where we changed into our dress clothes and returned to the main floor.

I put on a bow tie. I hadn't worn one since my wedding, so Philippa had to redo it for me. The older couple passed by us and laughed. We were in the corridor and had yet to go into the dining room. We were alone. Philippa was wearing a black dress. She had on a nice perfume and her hair was done up. Candles were burning and I glanced at her back reflected in the tall mirror behind her. The long, vertical scar there that was like a river to me.

My phone rang. I looked down at the screen but before I could put it away, Philippa snatched it from me.

Who's the Pythia? Philippa said.

I didn't know what to say. Not because I didn't want her to know but because I was stunned her mother hadn't ever told her.

The phone rang a few more times and then stopped. I promised I would tell her at dinner. Philippa raised an eyebrow, intrigued. There was something else I had wanted to say to her but it slipped away from me.

So I held her face. I kissed her brow, maybe for the first

time, and smelled the perfume on her and still the gunpowder. And we both grew shy about the kiss and peered into the candlelit room, where a group of musicians began to tune their instruments.

She took my arm. My daughter the river.

Lead the way, Philippa said. Let's go in.

AUTHOR'S NOTE

This book was written at the New York Public Library's Dorothy and Lewis B. Cullman Center for Scholars and Writers. I thank Jean Strouse, Lauren Goldenberg, Paul Delaverdac, Julia Pagnamenta, and all my colleagues there for their support, faith, and friendship.

Thank you to Matthew Chamberlain, Bret Anthony Johnston, Ethan Rutherford, and Nayon Cho. Christopher Beha and *Harper's Magazine*. Rob Spillman and *Tin House*. Allison Wright and *Virginia Quarterly Review*. Beth Staples, Anna Lena Phillips Bell, Emily Louise Smith, and *Ecotone*. Caroline Casey. Christopher Lin. Zachary Knoll, Loretta Denner, Amanda Lang, Jonathan Karp, and Simon & Schuster. Chris

Clemans, Henry Rabinowitz, Marion Duvert, Kirsten Wolf, Simon Toop, Hannah Hester, Drew Zagami, Jillian Buckley, and the Clegg Agency.

"Vladivostok Station" was inspired in part by the history of Sakhalin Island in the North Pacific Ocean. The geographies of certain locations—in particular Shanghai—were radically altered to suit the purposes of these stories. The actual Milner Field is located in West Yorkshire, England; the one in this book, which is in North Yorkshire, is pure invention.

Thank you, especially, to Marysue Rucci.

To Bill.

To Ralph.

And to my wife, Laura.

ABOUT THE AUTHOR

Paul Yoon is the author of the story collection *Once the Shore* and the novel *Snow Hunters*, which won the Young Lions Fiction Award. He is the recipient of a fellowship from the New York Public Library's Cullman Center for Scholars and Writers, and his work has appeared in *Harper's Magazine, Tin House, VQR, The O. Henry Prize Stories*, and *The Best American Short Stories*. He lives in Cambridge, Massachusetts, where he teaches creative writing at Harvard University.